BETHLEHEM'S BROTHERS

WRITTEN BY:

RONALD HERA

RECOMMENDED BY THE US REVIEW

Bethlehem's Brothers
by Ronald Hera

Book review by Kate Robinson

"And is this gift for gentiles and well as the Jews?"

Nine-year-old Simeon and six-year-old Enoch and their mother, Esther, survive the first-century AD Massacre of the Innocents in this young adult historical suspense novel, the first of a trilogy. The boys' youngest brother and their father are brutally murdered by Roman soldiers in the surprise nighttime mission. This horrific execution of all male children two years old and under in the vicinity of Bethlehem, as ordered by King Herod of Judea, is a measure meant to destroy Jesus, later known as Jesus of Nazareth, the long-prophesied Jewish Messiah.

Forced by fate to survive in a patriarchal world of simmering religious and cultural clashes, Esther must move through her grief and haunting memories quickly to find suitable apprenticeships for her sons because she cannot support them in Bethlehem without their father. Simeon is apprenticed to a former rabbi, now a potter in Jerusalem. Esther accompanies Enoch north, to Galilee, so he can learn the fishing trade with her brother-in-law, Lamech. As the boys' lives progress into manhood, there are sorrows and joys ahead as they seek out and witness the miracles of the prophet Jesus.

This adventurous tale meanders through a well-researched series of historical events recounted from the personal viewpoints of both historical and fictional figures. The characters are well-rounded and engaging, and their development is realistic. The many biblical stories in the novel are brought to vivid life. The down-to-earth prose flows smoothly, and the web paragraph format has room for notes if readers are interested in jotting down related Bible verses or other information. The novel could be used in classrooms as a companion for history or humanities studies and will enlighten young Bible study readers interested in understanding the mystery of the man known as Messiah and Savior.

Printed in the United States of America

Library of Congress Control Number:	2019920459
ISBN: Softcover	978-1-64376-717-8
eBook	978-1-64376-716-1
Hardback	978-1-64376-767-3

Republished by: PageTurner, Press and Media LLC
Publication Date: 04/15/2020

To order copies of this book, contact:

PageTurner Press and Media
Phone: 1-888-447-9651
order@pageturner.us
www.pageturner.us

Dedicated to my loving wife, Gerri

FOREWORD

Often people make the comment that they wanted to be there when Jesus was walking the earth. Here is your chance to experience it with Enoch and Simeon in Bethlehem's Brothers.

Their life begins in Bethlehem and with bloodshed. The Roman Empire occupies Palestine, and Caesar considers it of little consequence as long as his soldiers keep the peace. Peace is elusive though with zealots constantly seizing any opportunity to kill Romans and Harrod prepared to do anything to keep his throne.

Survival is paramount. Keep a low profile and don't rock the boat. But one came who rocked the boat big time. His arrival means conflict with both the Romans and the Jews. Here is one hunted from the time he was two years old and either hated or loved. The world needs a savior, but is he who he claims to be? Enoch and Simeon must decide, just as you must decide.

Three men on camels left the banks of the Jordan and traveled eastward through Decapolis. They rode their animals quietly but with faint smiles on their faces like men who had seen a miracle.

Chapter 1

"Wake up, Simeon, Romans are outside and trouble is brewing."

"Romans?"

"Yes, son, come with me and Little David to the mat in the corner," Esther whispered, "and be quiet." Then she dragged him across the cold dirt floor while clutching Little David in her left arm. She stuffed the baby into a camelhair blanket and shoved him into the corner muffling his sobs, then set Simeon down nearly on top of his brother and then faced them with her back to the door. She spread her arms and clutched the walls as if such a barrier would somehow protect her six-year-old and infant from all danger.

Simeon peeked around her to see the flickering light of the torches penetrate the cracks in the door and hover as if blankets set on end.

Simeon's father, Jacob, grabbed nine-year-old Enoch, set him on his feet and quickly pushed him into the opposite corner, their eyes wide in terrified anticipation.

Esther placed her hand under Simeon's chin, turned his face up, and then touched her index finger on her lips to insist on silence.

The family froze when they heard heavy beating on the door. Simeon continued to look up as his mother just stood there with her index finger quivering against her lips.

With a dull thud, the door swung open and crashed against the wall as if forced by a mighty wind, and the room suddenly became bright. Simeon peeked again as two Roman soldiers charged into the room and stood tall with their feet wide apart as the cool night air rushed past them. Both were blood splattered, and blood dripped from their swords. At once, they spotted Simeon's father in the far corner with Enoch.

The taller figure stood still in the doorway with a torch in his hand, while the light-skinned foot soldier with hair the color of ripe wheat and eyes as blue as the sky approached the helpless father and son. The Roman brandished his sword at Simeon's father as if to kill him, ignoring Enoch. The taller soldier shouted in a strange language and the soldier backed off.

Then he approached Esther. As he grasped her to turn her around, she rolled into a ball and fell to the floor shuddering with fear. That was more than Jacob could take. He lunged at the soldier and started to scream, "Leave them…!" But the well trained soldier turned in a flash and ran the cold metal sword through Jacob! Esther, Enoch and Simeon screamed in unison as the lifeblood gushed from Jacob. They rushed to his side, leaving the baby unattended. Little David just peeked out from under the blanket inquisitively. David was too young to understand.

The soldier looked down at David and swiveled toward his co-conspirator in the doorway who silently nodded. As David innocently looked up at the Roman, with one clean, low, sweeping motion, the seasoned killer sliced the head from Little David's body. The head fell to the floor and rolled to the feet of Simeon.

For an instant, David's eyes looked questioningly up at his brother then went blank. Simeon froze. To him, the world was a blur. This could not be happening to him in his little home, his quiet little hometown…. his peaceful world.

Simeon then heard his mother weep the same distant sobs that Simeon heard when he first stirred from sleep. She held her dead husband's limp body in her lap swaying forward and back as blood dripped from her sleeve. Enoch crawled to her side, looked at his father, his mother, his decapitated brother and then angrily at the men as they brushed the doorway on their way out into the chaotic street.

Simeon just stood in silent horror, and stared at his little brother's severed head.

***

That night the soldiers walked the few kilometers to the Herodium. The mercenaries silently peeled off to the barracks, while Marcus, their Roman leader, continued to the lower palace entrance at the foot of the mountain.

"Where is Herod?" asked Marcus as he met the guard at the door.

The guard signaled toward the pool without even a salute. Marcus walked the marble floors of the building to the pool area that always impressed him no matter how many times he saw it. It stretched over sixty meters wide and nearly seventy meters long and surrounded by gardens. The circular island with columns that stood in the middle of the pool was a common location for Herod and his friends, but he was not there. Marcus asked another of Herod's personal guards where to find the Governor. The guard led him to a guestroom heavily guarded by Herod's crack troops..

The guard left Marcus at the door, turned and addressed Herod through the doorway. "Marcus has returned, Your Excellency. Do you want to see him now?"

"Yes, show him in."

Herod was crouched like an animal over his strong wine. The scowl on his face reflected Herod's evil, crooked mind. Without even looking up, he immediately interrogated the officer. "Is the mission complete, Marcus? Is there any chance we have missed a single one of those stinking, little, Jewish animals?" Herod finally looked eagerly into Marcus' eyes. Marcus didn't dare to hesitate lest his head be lopped-off too.

"The mission is complete as you instructed, and all Bethlehem Jews under two are dead," Marcus replied.

Herod smiled with satisfaction and dismissed Marcus with a brush of his hand. With that, Marcus turned and headed toward the doorway. His outward demeanor was stoic, but inside he seethed. *What dirty, filthy work this is! Palestine is the most Godforsaken place on earth. How could anyone possibly believe that a two-year-old is a threat! I hate this place.* From that time on, he plotted to get himself out of Palestine.

Herod retired to his usual quarters, satisfied with the answers, but troubled by the feeling that he was still threatened by the "King of the Jews" supposedly born in Bethlehem. *Is he still out there? That dirty little "King of the Jews!" How can I know for sure? These bands of rebels I govern are crazy. They threaten Rome at every turn, and yet they are hopelessly incapable of ever freeing themselves of Roman rule. Why don't they cooperate? Why don't they accept their fate? Why don't they honor me? After all, I have brought great wealth to this barren land, and I have built so many beautiful buildings... like this palace! There is plenty of work for stonecutters, carpenters and artisans. Lots of money comes from Rome. Yet they leave every day for places like Egypt. Why?*

The Jews drove Herod insane. They made his stomach ache. If more bloodshed were necessary, Herod would not hesitate to kill them all.

Chapter 2

As dawn approached, Bethlehem awoke in the shadow of the Herodium. Grieving parents staggered into the street, aimlessly weaving, sobbing and wailing. Young men, appointed by the Rabbi, searched each home for the dead children and moved in quickly to carry them out and to bury them in individual graves. The sun was hot. The work was horrifying.

An elderly man came to Esther and quietly approached her. "Esther, we must take the boy and Jacob. I know this is hard for you, but we must. Rebecca is outside and will be with you while we take them out. You can come to the gravesite if you must, but it is a terrible sight. Come now. Let go of Jacob."

Esther tenderly moved Jacob's head from her lap to the hard, dirt floor and rose to her feet as she clutched the old man's arm. She looked over her shoulder at Simeon and Enoch but could not bear to look at young David's crumpled body. Enoch had covered the head to force Simeon to cease staring down at his little brother. Esther slowly staggered out the door into the light of day.

Enoch and Simeon stayed close as they shuffled out with their mother. Then Enoch suddenly turned and went back inside, picked up his father's prayer shawl, and joined the old man and the others who were collecting the fallen. Enoch's face was ashen and stern.

Simeon sat under the cypress tree with his mother as the old man and Enoch moved on. Esther was unable to speak. Simeon spoke to her, but her face was blank. Her dark eyes were unfocused and empty. Her blood-matted hair crinkled as she turned her head.

It frightened Simeon and he too became silent. He felt no hunger and no pain. Each time he closed his eyes he saw his younger brother gazing up at him with that questioning look. It helped if he only blinked.

Rebecca, a thirty-year-old childless widow, approached Simeon's mother and sat next to her. Then Esther turned and looked questioningly into her friend's eyes as a tear slowly rolled down her cheek. The supportive Rebecca lifted Esther back to her feet and held her as she sobbed silently, her whole body shaking with grief. "What will become of us?" whispered Esther.

How could one answer this new widow with two boys in a town with many other widows? Both women knew the future was uncertain at best, but now it was certain to be bitterly cruel.

Esther looked down at Simeon and reached out to him. Simeon rose to his mother's side and wept a flood of tears that only a mother's love could dry. Esther sat back down on the stone under the tree and lifted Simeon onto her lap. She held him close to her bosom as she had so many times before. She remembered happier times with Jacob and Enoch when Simeon was only a baby. Now he was her baby again.

Rebecca stayed for the entire day as other women moved about the town either helping or utterly dumbfounded. Rebecca knew she was needed at an hour like this, but how could she really help? She wondered why anyone would do such a thing. Even the Romans seemed more civilized than this. The soldiers were kind to Rebecca when her young husband fell from the scaffolding while working on the Herodium. *Can no one be trusted?*

Suddenly, Rebecca remembered Mary and Joseph. She had not seen them since yesterday and asked a woman passing by, "Have you seen Mary or Joseph and their little one?"

"They are gone," the woman replied. "No one has seen them. They escaped or something. We just don't know."

"Oh! I hope they escaped," Rebecca responded and then turned her attention back to Esther.

When Enoch returned, the petite Esther led her boys to the well and began cleaning the blood from her body, her clothes and her children. She tried not to relive the horror of the attack, but flashes kept streaming into her head. *What kind of person was the light-haired soldier from the West? They must have no respect for human life, no Yahweh whatsoever. Where do the Romans get such animals for their army?* Questions raced through her mind faster than she could comprehend them, let alone formulate any answers. All she knew was that the Romans had killed her husband and baby boy. A fever of hate began to well up in her body, consuming her whole being, and the need to shelter her sons became her obsession. She was a changed woman, bitter and protective.

Chapter 3

Having no relatives in Bethlehem, Esther recognized she could not make it alone. "My mother taught me to weave," she later told Rebecca. "But so can many of the others in town. I hate to sell to the Romans, but they are wealthy and have women to keep happy. Roman women cannot weave, nor can they do much of anything else for that matter. I know of Jacob's younger brother who fishes the sea in Galilee named Lamech, but I am not exactly sure where he lives in Galilee. Maybe he can help."

"Send a message to Lamech by way of a Canaanite trader. They are good at finding people and are not too expensive. They pass through here occasionally. You have seen them."

A few days later, Esther took Rebecca's advice and sent a plea to Lamech explaining her plight. A return message arrived in four weeks from Lamech.

Dear Esther,

How sad to hear of our loss. I grieve for my slain brother. I talked with my crew, and I am convinced that I can take only one of your sons. That is all I can handle. I have two small fishing crews, a wife and two young sons to support. I prefer to take the older son. He will be of more help to me and can begin fishing quickly.

I will send one of my finest men to Bethlehem to meet you and help you make the trip to Bethsaida. He should arrive five weeks after you receive this letter.

Lamech of Bethsaida

Esther debated for days about letting go of yet another son, but knew she could not continue to stay in Bethlehem. There were just too many haunting memories. She struggled for words as she explained Lamech's letter to Simeon. "I don't want to part with you, Simeon, but we must do something,"

Simeon didn't know what to say, but understood his uncle's answer. The idea of fishing for a living upset Simeon, but he knew he needed to learn *some* trade. Who would teach him? His father was a stonecutter. The last thing Bethlehem needed was another stonecutter, and Simeon knew it. His father's friends had taken in widows since that night, but it didn't work very well since women in town were all jealous of each other. Simeon wanted out of Bethlehem, so he spoke up, "Can I go somewhere else?"

Esther was surprised at the insightful answer her young Simeon offered. For the next three weeks, Esther struggled to find someone who would take Simeon. He and Enoch had worked with stonecutters and their father, but stonecutters only wanted carriers. Carriers were no more than slaves, and Esther was no fool. Finally Naomi, a neighbor, told her about her childless older brother, Thomas who was a potter in Jerusalem. He made a meager living but longed to teach his trade to someone who would appreciate it.

"He is older, fifty, and is running out of time. He will probably take Simeon if it is suitable to you, Esther."

Esther was relieved, but Simeon was not pleased. Jerusalem was the big city and Simeon wanted no part of it. He wanted to please his mother, and he realized he didn't have much choice. What options were there anyway?

Only eight days after talking to Simeon, a knock came at the door. Simeon started for the door, but Esther stopped him. Every knock at the door reminded her of the night of the slaughter. She peeped out through a crack in the door, and there stood a stout man with a well-kept, white beard standing beside Naomi. His face was wrinkled with age but not sundried as were most of the stonecutters in

Bethlehem. He wore a tasseled prayer shawl over his shoulders as if he wore it all the time, and he looked a little out of place in the small town of Bethlehem.

Esther opened the door slowly but said nothing.

Naomi introduced the old man. "Esther, this is my brother, Thomas."

"Shalom Esther," the man said with a tender tone in his voice. "My name is Thomas, the Potter of Jerusalem, and I have come to meet you and the boy. May we come inside?"

Esther opened the door and looked down at the dirt floor, for she could hardly bear being seen. The boys sat on the cool floor eating dates. Thomas entered slowly as Naomi followed.

Simeon looked up at Thomas. The man had a captivating smile and greeted Simeon with a look of joy. "You must be Simeon. My name is Thomas, and I have come to talk to your mother about you helping me in my pottery shop."

Simeon didn't reply.

Esther offered Thomas the bench along the wall as she stood in the middle of the room to speak with him. " we're glad you are here, Thomas. There is not much to say. My son has no real choice in the matter. He must work somewhere, and this is not a good town for him. Naomi

14

said you needed someone to help. You will not make a slave of him will you?"

Thomas smiled a gentle smile, sat down, took off his hat and laid it in his lap. Then with a soft voice he responded, "No, not in the least. I will train Simeon to take my place at the potter's wheel. Sometimes the work is hard. I will not lie. We work long hours, but the work is satisfying. My shop is the best in Jerusalem and my workers are good, gentle men. I believe Simeon will find it to his satisfaction. I only wish we were closer, so we could visit you and his brother more."

"We will not be here. we're going to Bethsaida in Galilee to be with my late husband's brother. That is even a greater distance, so I am afraid that this is goodbye to my youngest son."

Thomas frowned and gazed down at the floor. He knew it would be hard for Simeon and searched for words of comfort but came up empty. "Are you sure you want to do this?"

"We have no choice. My son is a good boy and he will do well for you. His father taught him respect and honesty. Now you must teach him a trade."

"I will do just that."

"Then we have a deal, Thomas the Potter of Jerusalem. We prepared for your visit, and Simeon is packed. Allow me a moment with my son, and he will be out soon."

"I have a few things for you outside. I will wait out there with Naomi."

Esther closed the door behind Thomas and turned to the boys. She drew both boys close to her and knelt down to look Simeon in the eyes. "Be a good boy for Thomas. He seems nice enough, and I trust Naomi's judgment. Give me a kiss, and then you must go." Simeon kissed his mother, and she hugged him one last time. Simeon looked at his older brother and gave him a long hug too. Then, like a soldier, he gathered his meager belongings and headed out the door with his mother and brother behind him.

"I have brought you as many pots as the donkey would carry. It will help you get along during this hard time." Thomas glanced down at the pile of pottery he had set on the ground for Esther.

"Oh, that is so kind of you. But what will I do with so many?"

"Sell them! It will help you to earn some funds for travel and settling any debts you may have. Naomi told me it has been hard for you and the boys. I wanted to help."

"You are indeed a kind man. Thank you so much. I am without words! Thank your wife for me."

"You have helped me greatly. I can now pass my craft on to your son. You have no idea how much that means to me. My wife passed away a few years ago, but I have the shop workers and some excellent neighbors there in Jerusalem who will help if we need it."

"I am sorry for your loss, Thomas. I will let you get started. I know it is a long way, and you must be tired. Take good care of my boy."

"I will. Come along, Simeon. We can get to know each other as we travel to Jerusalem. Have you ever been there?"

"No."

"I think you will like it."

"We will see."

Simeon listened attentively as Thomas described Jerusalem and his pottery works. He spoke of friends and neighbors who owned businesses. He told Simeon of the long hours of a potter and the hard work involved. Because of Thomas' pleasant demeanor, none of it frightened Simeon at all. In fact, the trip was an adventure and seemed idyllic as they traveled …the man, the boy and the donkey.

Chapter 4

The next week another knock came to Esther's door.

"My name is Nathan of Galilee. Lamech sent me. Is this the place of Esther, Wife of Jacob?"

Nathan was the escort from Bethsaida that Lamech had promised. He was a tall Galilean, about thirty-five years old with skin like leather. He was rough in appearance and frightened Esther a little. He was as opposite Thomas as possible.

"Yes, I am Esther. Do you have a letter from Lamech that I may see?"

"Here." He thrust the letter toward her so quickly that she took a step back.

"I see. My boy is with me and we have anticipated your arrival." Esther stepped outside to talk.

Nathan softened a little after he remembered he was speaking to a gentle woman and not one of his fishing crew. After the glimpse of the small room, he realized that here was a poor family with little else but a few pots. He was used to the larger home of Lamech and the openness of the lake. Although attractive, Esther appeared to be thin and her clothes were a little tattered. He hoped she could make the long trip to Bethsaida without difficulty.

Nathan casually checked the knife in his belt, concealed in the small of his back beneath his garment. He knew the dangers of travel and knew how to use the dagger. It had proven useful more than once. His assignment was to get Esther and the boy to Lamech. He was all business and liked it that way.

Nathan was pleased that Esther was also all business. He watched as she silently went about gathering the few belongings needed for the trip, leaving behind some pottery for her friend, Rebecca. The boy stood silently in the middle of the room and stared at Nathan. It made Nathan a bit uncomfortable, so he spoke. "And what is your name, young man?"

"My name is Enoch. Enoch, Son of Jacob of Bethlehem."

"Are you ready for a trip north, Enoch?"

"Yes sir, I am."

With that, Esther took Enoch's hand and closed the door behind them. Without speaking another word, they were on their way.

As they left Bethlehem, Esther turned and glanced over her shoulder. It was hard to leave the only town she had ever known in her adult life. Nevertheless, she didn't hesitate, realizing Nathan was moving at a quick pace like a man on a mission.

Nathan, Esther and Enoch moved quietly, kicking up the thick dust as they plodded along. The only time they hesitated was for a sip of water from the river mixed with a gulp of wine from the wineskins. Nathan helped the two tenderfoots negotiate past the puddles of the stinking donkey urine. Finally, Nathan gave them some instructions. "Be sure to let the camels and donkeys move along the inside of the path in the coming section. The path is narrow and the animals refuse to walk on the outside near the cliff. Stand still with your back to the valley. don't move. If you are too afraid to stand, just sit on the stones along the path. Don't startle the animals."

It became apparent why Nathan had warned them since it seemed hardly possible for a camel to pass between the mountain and themselves. Esther hoped no animals came along. They did only a few meters ahead of course and she had to deal with it.

Enoch, on the other hand, sensed a different danger. He didn't want to meet any Roman soldiers. His hate surpassed that of his mother and his reaction was different. She was afraid to disturb them or draw their attention while Enoch wanted to kill them, but knew he could not. He wanted to be strong, like Nathan. When they arrived in Galilee, he would ask how to fight and survive, and he figured Nathan would be glad to teach him.

Enoch had never ventured so far from home before, and as they hiked along the narrow dirt path, he gazed out at the countryside he was leaving. The brown, sandy soil beneath his feet spread like a blanket over the hills with just a few green dots to signal life. The rocks jutted out from the hillsides, and Enoch could only imagine what sort of animals might call them home. The sun was bright and the sky was blue with just a few wisps of clouds high above the cliffs. The beautiful day was a comfort to him.

Just a kilometer after descending into the valley of the Jordan, Nathan heard the faint chink of tiny pebbles rolling down from the cliff above. He turned to look west and the bright sun caught his eyes. Just then, a heavy weight hit him like a stone tumbling him to the ground. It was not a stone. He could smell the hot flesh of a man's body against his face. As he struggled to get out from under the man, a cold blade suddenly ran through his belly. Nathan kept struggling to escape, but his attacker struck him in the forehead with a heavy stone. Nathan fumbled for his dagger, grabbed its shank and thrust the blade into his assailant's side. The stranger screamed and cursed something in a strange accent as Nathan pushed hard and finally sent his attacker catapulting into the air. As blood streamed into Nathan's eyes, he rose to his feet, circled and searched for the man. The man had vanished!

Esther and Enoch were looking over the cliff as the man tumbled into the valley and struck the boulders below.

Nathan was hurt, and Enoch knew it. Enoch looked up the mountain, fearful that another attacker was near, but no one appeared. Esther stood in shock. It all happened so fast that she could hardly take it in.

"Nathan! Are you hurt?" shouted Esther, her voice revealing her terror.

"Of course he is hurt," Enoch shouted back with anger in his voice. Enoch grabbed the wineskin, took off his shirt to wipe the blood from Nathan's face and leaned him against the hillside. Enoch could see Nathan's injuries, but could also see scars from previous battles on his arms and body. Enoch quickly figured that Nathan could not walk out of this without some serious help.

"Please don't die," Enoch whispered in Nathan's ear as he sat him down. "*You* can't die too. Help will come. You'll see."

Nathan, squinting with pain, looked at the two of them and barked, "You have to get out of here. Others may be coming."

Esther stood her ground. "No! We have nowhere to go except on down the mountainside. We'll stay here with you." She handed Enoch her headscarf. "Here Enoch, wash his wound with the wine. Maybe a camel or donkey will come along. Not everyone is a killer in these parts. Elohim wouldn't let it be so."

Esther was right, but their savior was a surprise. The next travelers to appear were a small detachment of Roman soldiers, one on a horse. Marcus dismounted and leaned over Nathan. "Are you able to ride?" he asked.

Nathan slowly nodded yes.

"Here-- grab my shoulders, and I will lift you onto my horse. Easy does it now."

The foot soldiers positioned themselves along the edge of the path with their swords drawn, anticipating trouble. Alexander, the closest soldier, helped Marcus hoist Nathan up onto the skittish horse, and led him by the reins.

Esther and Enoch reluctantly joined the small group of Romans heading down the mountain path. Enoch was angry and confused. He only knew Romans as killers. To him, all westerners were killers, Roman or not. Proof of his opinion was just around the corner. A long row of makeshift wooden poles suddenly jutted toward the sky with the vestiges of men left to die by the Romans. Most were in various stages of decomposition. Birds, perched on the heads of fresher carcasses, pecked the eye sockets. The stench was sickening.

Esther knew of such things, but she had never seen it before. She stared up at the men on the poles and noticed empty spikes from other crucifixions. Some poles were empty, but none were without blood. She never spoke a word for fear of offending the Romans, and they never spoke either for fear of offending Esther.

The nearest town of any size was Bethany-Beyond-Jordan where there was an inn. "We will leave him here. Alexander, help him off the horse, and I will talk to the innkeeper," Marcus commanded.

Marcus barged into the inn like the Roman he was and shouted, "Get the innkeeper out here now!"

The elderly, bent-over innkeeper hurried the best he could to the door and followed Marcus. "What is the trouble?" he asked, thinking he had done something wrong.

"We have a man here who has been attacked and is badly hurt. I need you to take him in, and don't give me any excuses!"

The old man rushed back into the inn as two soldiers helped Nathan in through the rickety door. They plopped him on a bench and shoved him forward so his head rested on the table. A few of the patrons rose and moved along the wall with a look of horror. Marcus banged a small bag of coins on the table. "Here, this will take care of him for a while. Make sure you take good care of him. His wife and son are outside, and they will make sure you do. Understand?"

"Yes sir. I will do my best, but he is badly hurt."

"I have seen worse. Just do as I say."

"I will take care of him until he can travel again."

"Good. See to it that you do." Marcus turned and headed for the door. He took on a gentler tone when he approached Esther and said, "The innkeeper has promised to take care of your husband, you and the boy until he can travel again. I must move on with my men to Galilee. I wish you the best." Without waiting for a reply, Marcus strode to his horse, signaled to his men and headed out.

The innkeeper bandaged Nathan as best he could while Esther watched over him and wiped his brow. That night, Nathan ran a high fever and was delirious. He rolled in his sleep and flinched like a man struck by a whip. He drifted in and out of sleep for the next few days.

Finally, the fever broke, and Nathan could take a little water and seemed to be much better. He ate a little chicken soup and began to sit up. It was painful, but

Nathan was not one to complain. Esther heaved a sigh of relief when he began to talk coherently. She even heard him chuckle when she told him about everyone thinking they were a family.

Enoch paced outside, watching for more trouble.

Once the fever left him, Nathan seemed to recover quickly. After three days, he walked around a little and realized that, miraculously, nothing of importance was damaged. Two days later, Nathan paid the innkeeper a little more for his trouble and said, "I believe I am ready to head north with Enoch and Esther to finish my mission." The man with the scars and the strength of a bull impressed Enoch. From that day forward, Enoch and Nathan had the bond of man and son.

Travel was difficult and slow for the small company, but as they approached Galilee, Nathan seemed to possess new liveliness. His pace picked up and he gazed at the greener countryside and the lake with the admiration of a child. Esther and Enoch grew more relaxed and confident in their safe arrival. It certainly was an unusual trip.

The three arrived in Bethsaida just before the Sabbath. The fishing boats lay on shore with their nets draped over them to dry. The town of Bethsaida was just a little place about the size of Bethlehem. Lamech seemed surprised to see them since it had taken so long to travel from

Bethlehem. He had figured them for dead. Lamech also seemed distant as he pondered his new responsibility.

Lamech's young wife, Martha, was short in stature and plain in appearance. She greeted Esther and Enoch with a smile, then led them up a hill toward the house.

"Come in and rest your weary feet. It has been a long journey." She poured water into a large bowl, grabbed a cloth and began by washing Esther's feet. "I was beginning to worry about you. I thought perhaps you had changed your mind or met with an accident."

"We did have an awful experience. On the way, a robber attacked Nathan and Nathan had to fight him off! In the skirmish, Nathan was badly wounded."

"Nathan? Why, on earth, would a robber pick Nathan? He is one of the strongest of men. I believe that is why my husband sent him."

"Well, he certainly did well. The robber was no match for him."

The two women fell silent as Enoch excused himself. "I believe I will go look around, Mother." Esther nodded in agreement, and Enoch exited the home.

Once outside, Enoch went down the hill to the shore of the lake. He skipped a few rocks on the lake's surface and then walked to one of the boats. The larger crews required the larger boats so the boats varied in length considerably.

The largest boat was about ten meters long. All had a single sail rolled up on a horizontal pole lashed to the mast. The sides were made of boards sealed with pitch. Inside were all kinds of odd pieces of equipment. Other than the nets, he had no idea what the items were. He figured there was plenty of time to learn. Fishing on the beautiful lake surrounded by green hills might be interesting. In fact, Enoch had never seen so much water at one time.

***

A few weeks later Nathan sat on a large stone a couple meters from the shore of the lake and repaired nets. Lamech didn't seem interested in teaching Enoch to fish or even taking him out. As a result, Enoch sat by Nathan and learned how to repair nets. As they worked, Enoch asked Nathan, "Where did all those scars on your arms come from?"

Nathan raised his head slowly from his net and paused a moment. "I was a prisoner of the Romans and received lashes."

"Why did they arrest you?"

"They thought I was a Zealot."

Enoch was quiet now. He had heard of Zealots who ambushed Romans and slit their throats. Could Nathan do such a thing? He was certainly strong enough.

"My arms were tied above my head, and as they whipped my back they also hit my arms. The whip would wrap around my arm and as they pulled it away, it cut deeper. I thought they were going to dislocate my elbow, but it held, which is more than I can say for some of the others. One man even died."

"Was he a friend of yours?" asked Enoch, wondering how far he could go with this interview.

"No, I didn't know any of the others," Nathan responded as he lowered his eyes back to the net. Enoch took this as a signal that the interview was over, at least for now.

The next day Nathan and Enoch stayed home with the women and boys while Lamech went into town. Nathan was mending nets again as Enoch brought him the ones he found with holes. Nathan asked the questions this time.

"Enoch, do you have any idea why your brother and your father were killed by the Romans?"

"No."

"I think I know. Do you want to hear, or is this too hard a subject for you?"

Enoch replied with an angry look, "I think I *should* know."

"We think Herod ordered it because of something that happened in Bethlehem. Do you remember a group of rich men from the East coming into town looking for the King of the Jews?"

"Yes! They seemed to be friends of Herod. All sorts of strangers were in town. None of it made any sense."

"Well it doesn't make sense to us either, but we think they had something to do with this."

"Why?"

"Herod ordered all boys under the age of two to be killed, because he wanted to kill the 'King of the Jews' that night."

"You mean Herod and the Roman soldiers killed my brother because they were looking for a king? That still makes no sense to me. Why kill boys under two?"

"He believed the 'King' was a boy under two."

"That is ridiculous, Nathan. Who comes up with these things?"

"The Zealots do, Enoch."

Enoch looked surprised and frightened. "You said you weren't a Zealot!"

"I'm not, but I know some who are."

"Does this have something to do with the whipping?"

"Yes. The Zealots thought that because I was whipped, I must be one of them. So they talk to me now."

"Have you joined them?"

"No."

"Why not? It seems like that is the only way we have of getting rid of the Romans."

"I don't know, Enoch. I really don't know."

After a few minutes, Nathan offered. "Would you like to go out to fish tomorrow?"

Enoch thought for a moment. He liked spending time with Nathan. "Are you going?"

"I thought I would. I am tired of doing this. Aren't you?"

"Yes!"

"Well, let's plan to go fishing tomorrow," Nathan said with new enthusiasm.

The next day Nathan introduced Enoch to his crewmembers, Samuel and Jonah. Samuel was a tall, thin man, with short hair and a short beard, whose clothes hung on him like limp rags. Jonah, on the other hand, was very muscular. His eyes were set wide apart and his long hair gave him a somewhat frightening look.

As they pulled in the first net the excitement of the catch was exhilarating, and it was obvious that Nathan loved to fish. Nathan barked out orders as they handled the fish and in doing so taught Enoch the names of the tools of the trade. Enoch, in turn, was a willing worker and a quick student. In only a few weeks, Nathan regained his full strength, and Enoch felt like a real fisherman. The bonding was complete.

Enoch felt distant from Lamech, but it didn't matter much since Nathan was there. Lamech was busy running the family business and was more interested in getting the most for his catch than actually catching fish. Lamech's sons, David and Joshua, were little more than toddlers and not much help, but they were the sons of the owner, a wonderful position in life and envied by Enoch.

Chapter 5

Simeon and Thomas traveled to Jerusalem without incident. Thomas' donkey held bags with Simeon's clothes and three pots. On the way, Thomas stopped by a shop and sold the pots to the shop owner who greeted Thomas with enthusiasm. They were obviously friends.

"Who is your new friend?" asked the shopkeeper.

"This is Simeon, Son of Jacob from Bethlehem, my assistant. He is going to be the greatest potter in all of Judea," Thomas replied, matter-of-factly.

"I don't doubt it at all if you are his teacher, Thomas," replied the shopkeeper with a grin.

Simeon was a little embarrassed. He knew nothing about pottery, but he was encouraged by the shopkeeper's comment. Thomas must be good. The pots *were* better than any his mother owned when they lived in Bethlehem.

He picked up a pot and inspected it closely. Indeed, it was perfectly round, and the walls were of uniform thickness. The lines on the outside were fine and not as course as the lines on the pieces his mother purchased in Bethlehem. The bell at the top was larger, and he imagined it poured very well. Yes, it really was significantly better!

Simeon wondered if it was expensive and that was why his mother never had such pottery. He missed her already.

Jerusalem was full of people, just as Simeon had imagined. However, so many *strange* people surprised him. He noticed people with camels, apparently from far away, who bought and sold in the streets. Some had painted faces and were a little scary. Some were dressed in strange turbans and robes, while others were barely dressed at all. Shops were everywhere. They were small but neatly kept. Once he noticed some young women standing in a doorway of a shop with hardly anything inside and no windows. Simeon asked Thomas what they sold in those seemingly empty places.

"Actually, they don't sell much there," Thomas replied with a smile.

Simeon considered that a very poor answer, but figured he had plenty of time to learn about all the shops. He wanted to get to his new home and asked, "Are we almost there?"

Thomas smiled and replied, "We live just around the next corner."

They turned the corner and a pottery shop suddenly appeared. It was on the side of the hill just below the upper city. Outside the shop, all kinds of pottery sat on wooden shelves providing a safe, level place for the delicate merchandise. Simeon had never seen so many pots in one place. A young girl, about his age, sat among the wares with a grown man, apparently her father. Thomas greeted her, "Rachel, we're back!" Rachel rose to her feet. She seemed much taller than he anticipated because her legs were very long. She was thin with penetrating, brown, almond-shaped eyes.

"I sold a lot while you were gone!" she shouted with excitement. Her father smiled. Then she gingerly stepped over the merchandise and ran to Thomas. He hugged her in greeting.

"Thank you for your help, Rachel. I have no idea what I would do without you and Jared. Take your favorite piece back to your mother in exchange for your help." Turning to the man, Thomas said, "Thank you Jared, you are a wonderful friend."

Thomas motioned to Simeon, "This is Simeon, Son of Jacob from Bethlehem. He will be staying with me as he learns the potter's trade. Simeon, this is Rachel and her father, Jared. They live next door and watch the store when I am gone."

Simeon nodded to Rachel and said nothing. She looked *right* into his eyes, nodded back and also said nothing.

Jared said, "Hello Simeon." Simeon simply nodded again.

Thomas and Jared discussed the last week's sales. Jared was very businesslike and told him that they had sold seventeen pots, two large water vessels and six vases. It was apparent to Simeon that Thomas was satisfied with the sales.

Thomas then went to the back, tied the donkey to a ring on the wall of the shop, gathered some hay that was stacked nearby and fed the donkey. He then asked Rachel to draw some water for the donkey, Simeon and himself. Rachel placed the water pot on her head and gracefully strolled down the sloping street.

As Simeon and Thomas entered, Simeon noticed the mezuzah attached to the doorpost, a sign of a devout Jew. Inside, Simeon was impressed with the size of the operation. He met two sweaty workers, Irad and Seth, who greeted Thomas with fondness, making it obvious that Thomas was a well-liked manager. His shop was as clean and as neat as possible, with a large kiln glowing in the back and various pieces of pottery drying on shelves. It looked very complicated to Simeon and he wondered what

Thomas had in mind for him to do. He hoped it was not firing the hot kiln. It certainly looked ominous to Simeon.

Rachel returned with the water and placed it on the table. Thomas approved of the pot she had chosen for her mother and she skipped out the door without saying a word to anyone.

That night Thomas laid Simeon's mat out for him and sat down next to the mat. The light was dim and dust was in the air. The light coming through the cracks around the door reminded Simeon of that night the Romans killed his father and brother. The air seemed cold to Simeon but actually was quite warm.

Thomas spoke gently and quietly. "Simeon, I know this is hard for you. I believe you will find the neighborhood to be busy. The people here are hard working, just as your dad was. They are good Jews who know the scriptures well. We have traditions and ways of doing business here that may seem a little strange at first. I will teach you my trade, and you will find that it serves you well. We will start tomorrow and meet some customers. You also need to learn the scriptures. I will help you with that in the mornings before the shop opens.

"Can you read?"

"Yes, my father taught me some scriptures and how to read Hebrew."

Thomas was pleased, knowing that his job was much simpler than it could have been. Thomas stroked Simeon's head and watched him fall asleep. Silently, Thomas kissed the boy's head and then retired to his own mat. He knew that he and Simeon would have hard work ahead. Being a potter meant sacrifice and long hours. He prayed for strength and life enough to teach Simeon well.

Simeon slept fitfully that night. Dreams of his brothers and him playing in the narrow streets of Bethlehem bounced around in his head. Visions of Roman soldiers, agonizing cries and David's head interrupted his disconnected dreams. He dreamed of his father coming home from work and gathering all three boys into his arms, kissing them and saying how blessed he was. Simeon never made a sound as he tossed and turned.

Thomas was tired and was asleep before Simeon began to dream. The old man slept well, as the young boy tossed in his sleep.

***

The next morning, Simeon began his days with Thomas. The days were much the same for months to come. The "routine," Thomas called it. The day always started with Thomas putting on his prayer shawl ceremoniously and then kneeling with Simeon to pray for Yahweh's blessing on their home and the business. Sometimes he would include others, like Jared and his family, but mostly Thomas prayed for his business.

Simeon wondered if all the shop owners prayed in such a way, even Thomas' competitors, and if so, whom did Yahweh favor? It seemed odd to Simeon, because he never saw his father pray like this and had no idea what his father prayed about.

Next, Thomas took care of any special business before sunrise. The first day, he returned the donkey he had rented for the trip. The young neighbor seemed grateful for the money and bid Thomas a good, prosperous day. Thomas returned the remark and as they left the stable, grumbled something about highway robbery.

The scripture lesson started at break of day when Thomas asked, "Do you know any scripture, Simeon?"

"I only know bits and pieces that my father would quote."

"Say a few for me, so I know what you have learned."

"Uh…. 'Hear, O Israel: The Lord our God, the Lord is one. Love the Lord your God with all your heart, and with all your soul and with all your strength.[1] But those who hate him he will repay to their face by destruction; he will not be slow to repay to their face those who hate him.[2] My father used to say that about the Romans."

[1] Deuteronomy 6:4-5 NIV
[2] Deuteronomy 7:10 NIV

"Not bad. You know the Shema, but you have much to learn. You will start tomorrow by memorizing Yahweh's commandments brought down the mountainside by Moses."

Simeon could see concern in Thomas' eyes and felt stupid. Simeon despised learning scripture, but he knew most boys his age had memorized much more than him. He just wanted to get started learning a trade, and pottery making was fine with him. *Why all the fuss over a few words anyway? They are old and don't seem to be of much use for anything except to set rules and limits. The priests do all the talking to Yahweh anyway. What makes Thomas think he can talk directly to Yahweh? Is he just a little crazy? Yahweh will never speak to either one of us.*

The shop opened at dawn. At first, no one seemed interested in Thomas' wares. People passed and Thomas would call out to them while holding out a piece and promising a special price for them. When no one was nearby, Thomas named the various pieces to Simeon; wedding pots for the bride and groom's wine, and jars for carrying water from the well on one's head. Others were for wine and for oil or flat pans for bread. Decorated pots for special occasions and Jewish feasts dotted the ground. Pitchers with different kinds of spouts perched on makeshift shelves

Finally, customers began to take more interest and ask about various pieces. It was obvious when someone was serious about a particular pot. Thomas would sense that they were ready to buy and hand them an individual bowl or pitcher so they could inspect it closer as Thomas extolled its virtues. About half the time, they bought the piece after a little ceremonial bargaining. Simeon admired Thomas' ability to sell, and, obviously, he knew everything about all of his merchandise.

It was also obvious that people admired Thomas' work. Some would just stop, pick up a piece and look closely at it. Some would compare it with something at home and comment, "This is a lot nicer than ours." Others would give an approving nod to Thomas and move on. They knew he was a master. In fact, some called him just that! Simeon realized that it would be hard for him to match Thomas' work, but he had the promise from Thomas that someday, he, too, would be a master.

A few days later, Rachel stopped by and asked how it was going.

"About like any other day," Thomas replied. "For some reason, I think the customers like *you* better, Rachel." Thomas smiled at her with a sidelong glance.

She looked right back at him and said, "Of course!"

Simeon was out of the conversation with the exception of a glance from Rachel.

Then, suddenly, it became quiet. People stopped talking and milling about. They looked up the hill and moved aside. Simeon could hear the faint sound of a small bell, and he knew at once that it was a leper. His mother had warned him to stay away from lepers, and yet, she pitied them for their condition. Simeon had never seen a leper before but imagined a disfigured person with oozing sores all over his face. He strained to see. A faint voice called out "Unclean!" to warn others if they were unaware of oncoming danger.

A man in a tattered and torn garment slowly shuffled along, almost as if in a trance. As he approached the front of Thomas' pottery shop, he looked well to Simeon except for the sick-at-heart look on his face. Simeon turned questioningly to Thomas. Thomas whispered, "I'll explain after he is past."

As the man passed the pottery shop, he paused to look at Thomas as if he wanted Thomas to notice. Thomas nodded and then looked down. Simeon and Rachel looked at each other. It was obvious to both of them that Thomas knew this man! They wondered how it could be that Thomas knew someone like that.

After the leper passed, Simeon and Rachel looked at Thomas as if to ask for an explanation, but didn't speak. Thomas spoke quietly. "That was Josef, a fellow merchant who sold baskets. He apparently had sores on his body and went to the priest today. We know the diagnosis. I imagine it is what he thought, but hoped was not so. Now what will become of his family? It is hard to know. I didn't know him well, but I think he was a good man."

"So he is a *new* leper?" asked Simeon.

"Yes, we see them occasionally on this street, because the priest is just at the top of the hill. I wish he would move. It's bad for business."

"But what becomes of his wife?" asked Rachel.

"It is hard on the wives. No one wants to take them in, because they probably have touched him since he came down with the sickness. Sometimes brothers take them in anyway, but then the family that takes them in has a hard time until much time has passed. I don't even know if he is married. I am glad it is not our problem. We should pray for him tonight in our prayers, Simeon. Don't let me forget."

Simeon had never thought about the family of a leper before. *Would I associate with a friend whose dad had leprosy? Um, probably not.*

The crowd began to move again, but carefully choosing their steps. Gradually the street became nearly empty. Now Simeon could see what Thomas meant when he said the priest was bad for business, but in an hour, the street was busy again. It was odd, that an hour later everything seemed all right. The image of the man stayed in Simeon's head for the rest of the day. He honestly could not think of a worse fate.

As the weeks passed, Simeon became bored, and he looked forward to starting the work inside at the pottery wheel. He had inspected it the evening they arrived from Bethlehem, but was too tired to ask questions. Now seemed like a good time to interrogate Thomas about what they would do. Thomas dodged the questions artfully, and simply replied, "You will see." He finally added, "Pottery is an art. Not much one can say about it. You just have to experience it. we're, likewise, clay in Yahweh's hand to be molded as *he* sees fit."

Supper was a bore too. Just simple bread and beans cooked over a very small fire. Simeon knew he would miss his mother's cooking, but this was extreme! He could smell the cooking from Rachel's house, and it was much more to his liking. Maybe they would invite Thomas and him sometime. Finally Simeon asked, "Do you ever eat with others in the neighborhood?" hoping for a positive answer.

"I have on occasions," Thomas replied. "But the work requires that I get started as early as possible. Other merchants may count their money, even order more goods at night, but I have to make my pottery with the help of Irad and Seth. The basket weaver you saw with leprosy was in the same fix. It is not a glamorous life, Simeon."

It was not a very encouraging answer.

"Simeon, what is it at night that bothers you so much?" asked Thomas, changing the subject.

"Why do you ask?"

"You shout in terror some nights. Are you dreaming of that night in Bethlehem?"

"I don't want to talk about it. It is too terrible."

"You have to talk about it sometime, Simeon. Holding it in is bad for you."

"I relive it almost every night," Simeon replied with tears in his eyes. "I can't sleep well and I dread going to bed. I don't know what to do!" Simeon began to sob and shake.

Thomas was quiet for a while. He didn't know what to do either. He knew it would pass with time, but every time Simeon saw a Roman soldier, he stiffened and drew back. *Perhaps Jared would know.*

"Would you like to eat some good food for a change?" asked Thomas.

"Of course," replied Simeon.

"I'll see what I can do." Thomas rose from the pottery wheel as soon as he finished a small flowerpot. He walked away and returned in a few minutes with a broad smile. "We have a meal at Jared's tomorrow night!"

Simeon's mouth watered at the thought of a real meal. The food had not improved one bit since he arrived and every night he smelled the good cooking of Rachel's mother.

The next evening they closed early, and Irad and Seth went home to their families while Simeon and Thomas cleaned up for supper. Simeon was excited about the new adventure. He washed thoroughly and asked Thomas how he looked since there was no reflective surface in the shop. Thomas said, "You look like a handsome potter," and smiled. Soon that familiar aroma from next door drifted past them, and they grinned at each other in anticipation.

Thomas entered the house of Jared and quickly took off his worn sandals at the threshold. Simeon followed suit.

Jared came forward and welcomed them, "Rabbi, it is a pleasure to have you in our home, come, and sup with us." Such a formal greeting surprised Simeon. This was the second time that day someone smiled and greeted Thomas as "Rabbi." Jared caught a glimpse of Simeon's confused look, and then he looked at Thomas.

"You haven't told Simeon of your former self, have you Thomas?" Turning to Simeon, Jared explained, "We're old friends, Simeon. Thomas used to be a rabbi in the temple. I was his student…no his *favorite* student." Jared laughed and hugged Thomas. "He was a great teacher. Everyone loved him, and he taught us well. The

Sadducees didn't like his teaching though, because he taught of the coming Messiah and our life after death. Since the Sadducees do not believe in a life after death, they gave Thomas a pretty rough time, and finally those in charge pushed Thomas out of his teaching position. Now you know why we, who love him, call him Rabbi and greet him with such respect." Jared turned and looked at Thomas. "He is always welcome here."

They were barely in the door when Jared offered the explanation to Simeon. As they seated themselves around the low table, Jared took on a lighter tone and called to his wife Aiko. She came out to greet Thomas and Simeon with a bowl of hot water and towel to wash their feet. It surprised Simeon to see a woman much shorter than Jared, with the same almond-shaped eyes as Rachel and obviously not of Jewish descent. She was pretty, for her age, and Simeon decided that if she could cook and was pretty, she was fine with him.

Rachel entered the room carrying an open dish of fish and vegetables. She had a silver clasp in her ebony hair and looked directly at Simeon with those dark almond eyes of hers. She was beautiful. Simeon had never seen her like that before, and he tried not to gawk by finding something to catch his attention.

Then he saw the vase sitting nearby with flowers. It was shiny and white with a floral design outlined in gold.

It was smooth, tall, and beautiful. Simeon gazed at it for some time. He had seen nothing like it.

He looked at Thomas questioningly. Thomas said, "Don't look at me. It is impossible for me to create such a vase. It is from Aiko's homeland. Beautiful, isn't it?"

"Oh yes!" replied Simeon. Actually, he didn't know which was more beautiful the vase or Rachel. *What a night this is going to be! Good food! Good people! Even good pottery!*

Rachel and Aiko set the table, and Jared offered thanks. Simeon had never tasted such food before. The oddly spiced food had some new and strange vegetables. Aiko was definitely the best of cooks. Even his mother could not cook this well. As the night passed, Simeon ate and drank to his heart's content.

No conversation passed between Simeon and Rachel. Simeon talked only to the men and enjoyed Jared's humor and easygoing ways. Thomas was at ease with Jared, and one could see that they were great friends.

Jared asked, "Thomas, what do you think of the four new governors that Rome has appointed since Herod died?"

Thomas said, "I don't see much difference. Do you?"

"No, but maybe things will be more peaceful since Herod has been replaced by his offspring," offered Jared.

"I am not so sure. It seems to me that they are as nasty and evil as their father was. It is hard to believe that one man could produce so much evil. I am glad Herod is dead. At least he can have no more children!" Both men laughed.

As the evening wore on, Simeon became sleepy from the wine and bored from conversation he didn't understand. He occasionally dropped off to sleep, missing some of the conversation. Thomas used this time to ask Jared what to do about Simeon's dreams. Jared, however, was no brighter than Thomas about such things. They both decided that a good, busy job and time would heal the wound.

Finally, Thomas rose and said, "I believe we need to adjourn for the night and get to bed. I thank you, Aiko, for such a lovely meal, and thank *you* Jared for sharing your family with us. Come Simeon, we need to go." Simeon just nodded his usual nod to Rachel and slipped out with Thomas.

On the way home, Simeon never felt more relaxed and content. Once inside, he plopped down on his mat and fell asleep almost instantly. He dreamed that night of good food and good friends. He even dreamed of Rachel with her long, straight dark hair and alluring almond eyes.

***

The next morning, Simeon's lessons began with scriptures from the early books of Moses, but now

Thomas taught with new authority in Simeon's eyes. Simeon focused on what Thomas had to say, and he listened respectfully. What a difference it made, being taught by the best.

His pottery lessons began with handling the clay from the banks of the Jordan River. Thomas bought the clay from an old, skinny, white-haired man who only sold to Thomas. Thomas' shop had enough work to keep the old man busy, and he was a reliable vendor who delivered the damp clay with a coarse cloth covering.

Irad wet the clay twice a day and moved it to the wheel when Thomas was ready for more. Irad also moved Thomas' pots to the shelves for drying before being finished in the kiln. Irad appeared neat and wore the traditional beard well. Strong and well built, like Thomas, Irad didn't speak much; when he did, it was with a slight Samaritan accent. He quietly sang as he worked and would have been mortified to learn that the others heard his songs and enjoyed them.

"Watch for sticks, grass and pebbles in the clay, Simeon," he warned. "It is disaster for the clay. It will certainly ruin the product either in the making or the drying. Also, keep the clay moist all the way through. The only way to do that is to work it a little every day. It also allows you to check for pebbles and twigs. It doesn't sit on the shelf long before Thomas works it."

"What about the turned pots on the shelf?"

"They must sit for a long time. I always ask Thomas, he gives me the number of days, and I mark the shelf with the chalk for the day I give it to Seth. Thomas decides what turned pots and bowls go into the kiln together, and so I group them appropriately. You must be very careful with the soft clay. That is why we place them on the tiles. Never touch an undried piece!"

Simeon worked hard to handle the soft clay pieces and keep track of the days. It was actually quite challenging. Simeon worked for nine months moving the pieces and observing the days each piece took to dry. He saw the disastrous results in the kiln from every possible mistake. He made them all. Irad and Seth just took it all in stride and shared their own experiences. Apparently, they had made every possible mistake too.

Next, Simeon learned about the kiln. Seth tended the kiln. He located the hardwood for the fire, knew exactly how much to place in the kiln, and Thomas instructed him on where to place the pottery and how long to fire the product even though timing was inaccurate at best. Although it was extremely hot work, Seth loved his job and was the opposite of Irad in build and personality. Seth would joke and talk most of the day. His work didn't seem like the serious business it was to Irad.

"How long does it take a Roman to walk two kilometers?" Seth asked.

"I have no idea," Simeon replied.

"What about you, Irad?"

"Two Hebrews!" answered Irad. "You told that one last week."

Simeon laughed as Irad put his hand on his head and shook it in disdain.

"Well how about this one." Seth held up a finished water jug. "If I fill the jug to here, what do I have? Irad, you first."

"It is half full, I suppose."

"What about you, Simeon?"

"I say…. half empty."

"Now we ask Thomas the great potter of Jerusalem."

Thomas grinned and stroked his beard. Narrowing his eyes, he gave his answer. "The jar is twice as big as it needs to be. Let me sell you a smaller jar!"

All of them laughed as Seth added, "At a special price, I suppose."

Thomas would never allow Seth to converse with the customers regarding sales. He would give away the shop to learn a new riddle!

Simeon spent twenty weeks with Seth, and they became the best of friends. The riddles kept Simeon from thinking of his dead father, his mother and his brother. The loneliness seemed to leave him during his time with Seth.

Finally, it was time to work with Thomas and the wheel.

The wheel was heavy and was really two stone wheels, one above and one below. The bottom kick wheel used foot power to propel a vertical wooden shaft to the upper wheel. The upper wheel provided the platform for the clay. Thomas was an artist at working the wheel and it was no wonder he was so strong. His arms were strong from holding his hands steady while working the clay on the wheel, his hands were strong from forming the clay, and his legs were strong from pushing the kick wheel. The coordination was phenomenal to Simeon, but it was this work that Thomas wanted him to learn.

At first, the wheel and clay were in awkward positions for Simeon who was shorter than Thomas was, although only slightly. As time passed, Simeon grew, and the task seemed to shrink. Carefully, over the next five years, Thomas taught Simeon to mold the clay with deft precision. Simeon asked questions so he would understand the behavior of the clay.

"Does all clay behave pretty much the same, or is there a great difference when the clay comes from somewhere else?"

"All clay is different, Simeon. There is hard clay, soft clay and clay that just falls apart on the wheel. I like what we use because I am used to it, but there are better clays that come from the Nile and other places too far for us to use. The clay we get comes from a certain part of the Jordan, and the old man with the white hair, Nathan of Gilgal, digs just so deep. Beneath this clay is darker, harder clay, but it is too hard to work, I would be exhausted in a couple of hours. He knows just what to get and is an artist in his own right. One of the reasons we do so well is that we use just the right clay, and we owe Nathan for that. I pay him well, and he is an important part of our business although you seldom see him."

Thomas was amazed at how quickly Simeon understood. Now if only he understood the scriptures like he should.

Herod Antipas ruled Galilee tightly. He loved to be entertained and often at the expense of the entertainer. He was, in reality, more evil than his father was.

Chapter 6

Lamech stayed up late doing paperwork for the fishing business. When Martha and the others were sound asleep, Lamech threw a wrap over his shoulders and silently slipped out of the house. He hiked out of town to the top of a steep cliff and grabbed a rope tied to a nearby olive tree. He threw the end of the rope over the rim and lowered himself down to a small opening in the cliff. Inside the small cave, three other fishermen sat in the dim, flickering light of one candle. They looked up at Lamech and greeted him with only a nod. The oldest one asked, "Did you get a look at them?"

Lamech nodded, "Yes" and began. "Nearly twenty of them are camped a little east of Capernaum. They came north from the Herodium just over a week ago. My sister-in-law saw them on her way here with Nathan, but I have not asked Nathan about it."

"Why not?"

"You know Nathan. He just wants to fish and be left alone and will not help us. He is afraid of another Roman whipping," Lamech responded. "I tried to eliminate him on the trip back from Bethlehem, but failed. He is a tough one. In fact, he killed the agent I sent to kill him. He will never be of any help to us!"

"Someone needs to enter the camp and look around. We need to know their comings and goings, or how else can we surprise them?" asked a stocky man sitting in the background leaning against the wall of the cave.

Lamech stroked his short, stubby beard and thought a minute. His dark eyes formed narrow slits as he considered options. He knew a child was the best bet. The soldiers would be leery of a man wondering about for no reason. Zealots had lied when giving a reason to be in a Roman camp before, with disastrous results. The image of Enoch kept coming into his head, but if his wife found out he used Enoch, she would surely kill him in his sleep. Nevertheless, Enoch could do it! He was bright, hated Romans, and he was about the right age to pretend to be interested in their armor and could even make friends with them.

"I have some ideas; let me think about this a little while," Lamech stalled. "Nathaniel, you fish near their camp for a while, and then see if they have any boats or a way of moving south without drowning. I will talk to my nephew and see if I can recruit him for a mission into their camp. We will meet again in one week at sunset in the old fishing hut. Got it?"

They all nodded. Nathaniel left first. Then, they all climbed out one at a time, spaced over an hour.

The next afternoon, Lamech finally showed sincere interest in Enoch and asked if he wanted to fish with his crew for the evening.

"Of course," Enoch answered with excitement. He loved to fish with Nathan's crew and wondered if Lamech's crew was any different, and if so, how. He ran to Nathan and told him that he would be fishing with Lamech's crew that evening and wished Nathan a good catch. Then he ran back to Lamech's boat and climbed aboard.

As they shoved-off, Nathan looked out at the boat with concern in his eyes, but he spoke nothing of it to his crew. Nathan's crew missed Enoch since he had become such a good helper.

Lamech and his crew moved out onto the sea and chose a fishing spot near the east shore. The evening was beautiful with a red sunset, and the northwestern breeze was perfect for sailing. The boat rocked back and forth with a gentle rhythm that only the sea can create. Lamech stood next to Enoch and made light conversation until they threw the nets, and as they drew the first nets, Lamech asked, "Do you like to fish, Enoch?"

"Oh yes, very much," Enoch answered as he tugged on the net.

"I like to fish too and often pretend the fish are Roman soldiers being pulled in for the slaughter." Then he laughed.

Enoch joined him in laughter and nodded at a big one and said, "That is the leader." The whole boat crew laughed and then Lamech looked serious.

"Do you often wish you could do something to get back at those who killed my brother and your little brother David? We have something in common, you know."

"Yes. It makes me furious that I don't know how to handle a weapon. They could kill me in a second, just as they killed my father. We have nothing, and I am still small for my age, but the fishing helps me grow stronger. I tire of waiting for my chance."

"Chances are made, my boy. Chances are made."

They tugged at the nets. It was a good catch for the first hour. As the evening progressed into night, Lamech refrained from asking any more questions about Enoch's feelings concerning Romans. He had his answer. The recruiting would only take a couple of days. A few days of training and Enoch would be ready.

Late that night, Enoch sat by Nathan as he usually did and told of the evening's fishing. Nathan showed reserved interest and was generally quiet.

After breakfast the next day, Lamech and Enoch went for a walk outside while the air was still and cool. Lamech looked at Enoch and said, "We Jews are as numerous as the stars, and yet the Romans dominate us. If we all did just a little, eventually we'd defeat them and drive them from our homeland."

"It seems that way, but they sure have a lot of weapons that we don't have."

"Well, Enoch, weapons aren't everything. We could defeat them with cunning and deal them so many small losses that they would find it unprofitable to be here. Why bother with a bunch of crazies when they can go back to Rome and live in peace and luxury?"

"How could we do that?" Enoch asked.

"Just split off small detachments, poison them or something that doesn't require a lot of weapons, and let them rot. Maybe raid their storehouses, steal their horses and weapons and pose a threat. Then we could lead them all over the countryside, or world, and drive them crazy until they tire of it. We'd have enough of their own destructive weapons to cause them to fear us and leave us alone. Who knows, we may even take Rome someday."

"Wow! Sounds like you have given this some thought, Uncle. My father never thought of things like that. Do you really think we could do it?"

"If enough of us helped, I think we could, Enoch. I think we could."

They walked on in silence thinking of what could be.

Two days later, Enoch approached Lamech after breakfast as Lamech recorded the value of the previous night's catch. Enoch looked at Lamech. "I want to make it happen. You know, us and the Romans, like we were talking about the other morning."

"What are you saying, Enoch?"

"I am sure we could make it happen," Enoch whispered with enthusiasm.

Lamech said, "I will consider it, and maybe I can do something too, but keep quiet about these thoughts because the Romans and their spies would not approve. Tell no one, Enoch, and I mean *no one*. This must be our secret. Do you understand?"

Enoch nodded, excused himself and went to join Nathan mending nets. Lamech smiled. *Well, that was easy. I can introduce him to the others now.*

Four days later, neither Lamech nor Enoch went fishing. Lamech told the others that he was going into Bethsaida to introduce Enoch to some of the other businessmen and that they would be back after dark. Lamech and Enoch did just as Lamech had said until sunset. Then they made their way toward the Jordan River to a small, abandoned fishing hut about one hundred meters north of the sea. Intended for boat repair, it was empty except for tools. Nets stretched overhead from beam to beam on top of oars, a rope hung down at the far end of the hut and strange red paint marks identified three vertical boards of the back wall.

Soon, the others came, and Lamech introduced Enoch to the same men who had met earlier. They sat on the floor, and Lamech gave his familiar speech.

"We all know that the Romans have conquered lands all over the world and influence kings they haven't even conquered. Yet the conquered outnumber the Romans as the stars outnumber the hills. Something must be done, even the smallest thing, to begin the defeat of the Romans and drive them back to Rome like dogs to their den. They are weak without their technology, weak without their weapons, weak without their puppet kings, weak without their chariots, and weak without their numbers.

"A small detachment of Roman soldiers is camped nearby. Their escape is cut-off by the sea, and they are few in number. We need to know their comings and goings, we need to know what they eat, we need to know when they sleep, and we need to know how long they will be here before they move on. Who is man enough to find out for us?"

At this point, Lamech expected Enoch to jump up and volunteer, but he did not. The others knew the game.

The fisherman named Nathaniel spoke first, "I would, but they would suspect me. Why would a fisherman wander into the Roman camp, except to spy? I have no reason to be nosing around! We all have the same problem. They will be suspicious of us, except maybe of him." He nodded at Enoch.

"The mission is dangerous and besides, Enoch is not trained for such a thing," responded Lamech.

Enoch rose and said, "I can learn!"

With that, Lamech and the others explained to Enoch their individual roles as Zealots resisting the Romans at every turn. The troops in the area offered an opportunity for the Zealots to thwart the Roman mission, whatever it was. They needed someone to win the Romans' trust and Enoch was their most likely candidate.

Enoch felt excited and frightened at the same time. His palms began to sweat and he feared sweating all over. *How can I do this? Will they really accept me? What have I gotten myself into? If Mother finds out, she will chain me to a post. I want to talk to Nathan but can't.*

Lamech demanded complete secrecy.

Chapter 7

Marcus called to his scout, "Anthony!"

Anthony entered his tent and reported with his usual reply, "At your service, sir."

"Anthony, do you know what our mission is here?"

"No sir."

"Our mission is to find the Zealot terrorists who live in these parts and to destroy them. I need you to operate as a local and find out all you can about their routine. I will work with the men to station sentries around the clock guarding the camp. Because we can trust no one, we must be especially careful. Although this looks like a safe area, it most certainly is not, and I suspect some of the fishermen are fishing for more than fish. They are fishing for Roman's to kill."

"I understand," Anthony replied.

"Then tomorrow, I want you to go along the north shore here and find out how the fishing business is done in these parts; who buys, who sells, and who hunts Romans."

"Yes, sir," Anthony saluted smartly, turned, and exited the tent.

Twenty-year-old Anthony was of slight build and ruddy complexion. His abilities as a combatant were limited, but his ability as a scout was dazzling. He could spot a moving object in his peripheral vision without ever moving his head and then identify and describe what he saw in minute detail. Marcus trusted his judgment as much as his powers of observation. There was no one else he would trust to travel alone with so little instruction. Marcus knew he would receive a meticulous report.

Anthony walked through the camp wondering just how he was supposed to pass as a local. Finally, he entered his tent stripped and began rummaging through his clothes for something that was not obviously Roman issue. After pulling out a hideous robe, he slipped into worn out sandals to make him look both poor and of poor taste. Then he set out for some shopping in Capernaum.

While walking to town, Anthony just looked around. He counted the boats, recording their location and size. He noticed crews of three to seven to a boat, and he noticed that it was always two or more who worked on mending nets. Seldom did he see a fisherman alone. He concluded that they were a tight community of men who had worked together out of necessity for so long that now it was natural for them. They also had a common enemy, their oppressor, the Romans. Rome was their natural enemy treading on their sacred ground. He could immediately see why this area looked so innocent but was so dangerous.

In Capernaum, Anthony bought local clothes matching those worn by the sales people he saw in the shops. He knew that the fishermen would not immediately accept him because they would all know each other. The only thing he could hope for was a reluctant acceptance of an outsider. After changing clothes in a little uninhabited boat repair hut, he walked along the shore closer to the bank and greeted a few fishermen with a nod. Most of them greeted him back, but a few looked suspiciously at him and then went back to their work.

Finally, he stopped at one of the boats. An older man and his two young sons were repairing a broken board on their boat and needed another hand. Without saying a word, Anthony grabbed one end and helped pull the old board loose. After ripping the board loose from the hull, they all wiped sweat from their brows and the old man introduced himself in a thunderous voice as Zebedee. He introduced his two young sons, James and John, common names for those parts.

"I am Amos, son of Simon from Jerusalem." Marcus used a real name but one Zebedee was not likely to recognize.

"Greetings Amos. What brings you to the shores of Galilee?"

"I trade imported goods, mostly metal. You know... things that seem a bit unusual. I need to establish some more customers and thought perhaps the fishermen around the Bethsaida area may need some specialty items. Do you know of anyone who may need something that they can't get from around here, tools maybe?"

"I could use a saw, but I don't think you can get one quick enough to satisfy me," Zebedee thundered with a hearty laugh.

Anthony liked Zebedee immediately. "Who buys odd tools that are not common around here? That person would be my best bet for a new customer."

Zebedee looked up and stroked his beard thoughtfully. "Perhaps Lamech is your man. He has two crews and buys many things that I have no idea what he uses them for. They seem to have no possible use. I think he just likes gadgets."

"Great! Where can I find this Lamech?"

"He usually fishes just below the inlet, but I am not sure exactly where he lives. Just ask around and someone will show you who he is."

"Thanks and good fortune on your boat."

As Anthony walked away, Zebedee turned to James and John and said. "Now there is a man not to be trusted. He dresses like us, says he is a trader from Jerusalem, and speaks with a slight western accent. No, I think he is something other than what he appears. Be careful of such characters, my boys. Be careful. Before you associate yourselves with someone, you must be able to spot the real thing when you see it."

As Anthony hiked back to camp, he spotted something that surprised him. There, squatted on a rock, was the boy he had seen when the troops helped the injured man on the road to Galilee. Of course, he could not approach him, and say he was one of the soldiers. Therefore, he just looked at the boy as he mended nets and wondered if all was well with the family.

The sun had set by the time Anthony reported to Marcus. The first day was not very productive, but he was sure that in time, he would find some unusual activity that required closer investigation. "Perhaps Lamech is a key," he said. Anthony had no idea how right he was.

Marcus slept fitfully that night, dreaming of boats, fishermen and swords.

Enoch slept with his teeth clenched as he dreamed of avenging his father and little David.

Chapter 8

Lamech trained Enoch well. He knew what to say to the Romans and what not to say. He knew how to approach an officer and not give away the fact he was trying to learn their plans. Lamech knew it was risky for Enoch, but simply didn't care what happened to him.

Nathan suspected Lamech was up to something and checked it out with his Zealot friends. He finally found Nathaniel and learned of Enoch's involvement.

Nathan approached Lamech. "How could you do this to your own brother's son? Your sons know nothing of this because you protect them and Martha, but you risk Enoch like a worthless stone! You are a crazy man! You place no value on this boy, and besides Enoch is not yours to manipulate!"

"You stay out of it Nathan! You are a worthless stone yourself. You have no position on anything. You are a worthless Jew if you refuse to help us. You know that!"

"If anything happens to Enoch, his blood is on your hands, Lamech! And you will answer to me for a change!"

Nathan turned to go to his boat and crew. The crew knew exactly how Nathan felt about violent Zionists and Nathan had managed to keep them out of the Zealot camp. Their allegiance was to Nathan, not Lamech.

Lamech enjoyed the income that Nathan and his crew provided, but this was the last straw. Lamech renewed his determination to kill Nathan before the Harvest Feast.

Chapter 9

Finally, it was time for Enoch to make contact with the Roman troops. Enoch became a helper for the half-blind man who supplied the wood for the ironsmith's fire. He quietly delivered wood for a few weeks and finally approached the ironsmith who forged the weapons and tools for the detachment. "My master needs to know how long you will be here and need the wood."

"We will be here only a few more weeks. I have nearly enough wood to last until we leave. Tell your master to deliver two more times. Then I will have enough. Now be on your way!"

Enoch obliged him and left immediately. He reported to the gang that time was running out, and he needed to know what to do next. Lamech and the others decided to target the officer-in-charge. The detachment would leave with one less Roman leader. They asked Enoch to approach the officer and no one else.

Enoch delivered a small load of wood three days later and asked if he could have a drink of fresh water. He claimed his family was near starvation, and he didn't know what to do.

The ironsmith led him to the water and watched as Enoch drank. "Where do you come from, boy?" asked the ironsmith.

Enoch said, "I come from the other end of the lake and walk a long distance to carry the wood, but it is the only job I can find. I hope, some day, to go to Rome and join the Roman Army, like you."

The ironsmith looked surprised. "Are you able to leave? Sometimes we pick-up helpers along the way, and you look like a strong lad. Here, let me take you to Marcus." With that, the ironsmith led Enoch exactly where Enoch wanted to go.

A tall, foreboding sentry stood outside Marcus' tent and asked, "Who is this you have with you, and what do you want?" The ironsmith paused a minute wondering if this was a good idea after all. Then the guard called to Marcus, and Marcus came out of the tent to meet the ironsmith and Enoch. Marcus never allowed anyone to enter his tent.

One look and Marcus knew who the boy was. He also knew that Anthony had mentioned seeing the boy fishing near the mouth of the lake talking to the prime suspect, Lamech. However, Enoch didn't recognize Marcus. In the excitement of the attack along the road and because of his fear of Romans, Enoch had never looked Marcus in the face.

Marcus asked Enoch, "What is it you want, young man?"

Enoch replied, "I am from a poor family in the south and need something to do that would bring me some food and protection. I wonder if I could join the regiment." Enoch asked.

Marcus paused. "What would you do?"

The ironsmith quickly recounted what Enoch had been doing and said he could help him with the armor. Marcus agreed, but he asked Enoch to return in two days.

Enoch left feeling elated. Lamech would be so pleased.

✳✳✳

Anthony silently followed Enoch to the boat repair hut and crouched low behind some thick shrubs in the shadows. He observed the men enter one-at-a-time, until all six were inside. He quickly rose and retreated three hundred meters to a waiting sentry and asked the sentry to have Marcus assign a man to follow each of the six to their homes. "The soldiers must keep their distance," Anthony whispered. Later, Anthony himself followed Enoch and Lamech to Lamech's house.

Near the house, Nathan was reclined along the shore leaning against a bank watching the moon drift across the lake. He was nearly asleep when he heard Enoch and Lamech walk up the bank. He knew it as late and was a little concerned that Lamech was keeping Enoch up so late. Then he noticed the faint reflection of the moon's rays about fifty meters behind them. Startled, he sat up to take a closer look, but the reflection was gone. He waited and watched, but it didn't reappear. He made nothing of it and went back to his quiet spot along the shore.

Enoch entered the house and plopped down on his mat.

"Where have you been, Enoch? I haven't seen you for a day and a night."

"It is men's stuff, Mother."

Esther grabbed Enoch by the nape of the neck and looked unflinchingly into his eyes. "Anything you do is *my* business. I have lost one son and I am *not* about to lose another, so you tell me what is going on! You are out too late to be doing '*nothing*'."

"I have been with Nathan along the shore planning a fishing trip further south than we usually go."

Esther didn't accept the story but knew she could check with Nathan in the morning. Both went to bed angry.

The next morning, Esther spotted Nathan rinsing out the boat and sauntered down the hill toward the shore. Nathan could see immediately that she was not a happy woman.

"Nathan, Enoch tells me that he was with you late last night sitting up and planning fishing trips to the South. Is that correct?"

"No."

"Then why is my son lying to me?" she demanded.

"How would I know? I hardly talk to the boy anymore."

"Well he is up to something, and I don't like it."

"I'll talk to the boy. I will make sure he goes with us this evening," Nathan offered.

Esther walked back toward the house, seething.

Quickly, Nathan turned to Samuel. "Samuel. I want you to go into town and buy another order of pitch for the boat and bring it back right here to the boat. Then wait for me here on the shore."

"We have plenty of pitch."

"Just do as I say! You know half of what I say doesn't make sense anyway. Just add this to your list. Here take this." Nathan tossed his purse to Samuel.

Samuel shook his head, mumbled something and set out along the shoreline toward town.

Nathan approached Lamech. "I need Enoch badly this evening. Samuel is in town, and I need his help."

Lamech was staying in that evening anyway, and he didn't care which boat Enoch was on. "Sure, take him." He waved his hand in resignation.

"You will fish with us this afternoon," Nathan said as he passed Enoch on the way to the boats. Enoch looked pleased and started to gather his gear. Nathan looked at him and then watched Lamech walk toward the house as the other boat headed out. He sensed trouble and wondered how he would get Enoch to speak openly while fishing. "You look tired, Enoch. Been up late?"

Enoch sensed the interrogation coming and simply answered, "Yep." He was determined not to talk much for fear of giving away his late night activities.

Onboard the fishing boat, the evening seemed long and boring to Enoch. Nathan remained quiet until he formulated an opening line. Then, out of the clear blue, Nathan commented. "I saw you at the boat repair hut last night."

"So?"

"I know those people, Enoch."

"So?"

Jonah was growing uncomfortable but went about his business without a glance away from his work.

Nathan grabbed Enoch and Enoch struggled to get free. Nathan's iron grip was far too much for Enoch, and Enoch settled down but with a look of fire in his eyes. "So… they put us all at risk. Do you know what Romans do to Zealots? They kill the whole family. Your own mother is at risk. I am at risk. Samuel and Jonah are at risk. I want to know what is going on and I want to know *NOW*!" Nathan's voice echoed across the lake.

Enoch had too much respect for Nathan to hold back any longer. "The detachment at the north end of the lake. I go there tomorrow to kill their leader, Marcus."

Nathan was visibly shocked. "Just like that, you are going to kill Marcus. Do you know who Marcus is? Answer me, boy. Do you know who Marcus is?"

"He is their leader, that's all I know and all I need to know."

"You idiot! He is the one who saved me along the road. I owe my life to that Roman! Besides, you don't just walk up to a Roman officer and kill him. For heaven's sake, boy, your own uncle is sending you to your death. And your mother's death! Quick, Jonah, back to shore!"

Lamech's crew had no idea of the conversation. They only heard Nathan yell "*NOW*" and knew trouble brewed. When they saw Nathan's boat pull in the net, turn about and head for home they all stood and stared at the boat, then looked at each other in bewilderment.

Jonah and Nathan jumped out of the boat as it slid up onto the sandy shore. Samuel had just returned and Nathan shouted, "Get in the boat, all of you! Now push off!" Nathan left the boat as Samuel hopped in. Then Nathan ran toward the house. Lamech came out with a look of bewilderment on his face. Nathan ran to him and knocked him cold with one blow then called, "Esther! Esther!" She came running out with Martha.

Martha ran to Lamech, bent over him and looked up with anger at Nathan, "What is going on here?"

Nathan ignored her, ran to Esther and took her in tow. "Come with me, now! No time to talk!"

Just then, Anthony and the other troops began their descent toward the lake with swords drawn. Nathan and Esther began running toward Capernaum, hoping to disappear there. Two soldiers split off, at Anthony's command, to chase Nathan and two others headed toward the boat. The rest of the soldiers headed toward Lamech's house.

There was no battle. Lamech was out cold on the hillside while Martha and the boys ran inside but to no avail.

"Get them all!" commanded Anthony.

Lamech's crew had followed Nathan's crew and found themselves in harm's way on the shore. Hurriedly, they began to push their boat back into the water. "Quick!" shouted one.

But it was too late.

Lamech's crew threw nets and tackle at the Romans, but it just bounced off their shields. In a matter of minutes, the soldiers pulled the rope attached to the boat, and the fishermen tumbled backwards, off their feet. They were helpless on their backs. The Romans boarded the small fishing boat and one-by-one ran them through.

Samuel, Enoch and Jonah were safely on the water.

Anthony turned and gave chase for a short distance toward Nathan and Esther. Then he stopped and shouted, "Get news to Marcus to round-up the other Zealots. Somehow, they know we're on to them."

The appointed messenger sprang into action ascending the hill toward the makeshift station Marcus had set-up for this very purpose. Marcus and four others met the messenger and donned their helmets.

The small fishing village was terrorized. The soldiers knew exactly where to go. They crashed in the doors of the families of Lamech's fellow Zionists and killed everyone inside leaving their bodies where they lay. The carnage was quick and sure. No one escaped the wrath of the Romans. When done, the soldiers quickly marched to camp, expecting the soldiers who had chased Nathan to be there to meet them, but they were missing.

Marcus ordered Anthony to take four men and go to Capernaum. When they arrived, the town was quiet again with no sign of a struggle. Anthony questioned a few frightened townspeople concerning the whereabouts of any Roman soldiers and was told that Roman soldiers were all over the town. Then they moved eastward from the town back to Lamech's house. There was no sign of the soldiers there either.

Anthony and the others were baffled about how two soldiers could disappear so suddenly. They returned to Marcus with the news.

Marcus thought for a moment. *They are probably dead in the lake. I traded two of my best men for the Zealots. Not a good trade, but we will have to settle for it.* Then he spoke, "Our work is done here, and tomorrow we leave this place and move to Jerusalem. Tell the men to prepare to break camp."

Nathan and Esther were unscathed. Nathan had tricked the two soldiers into following them into the hut used by the Zealots. There was a trap already set for just such a situation and Nathan knew it. As the soldiers broke down the door, Nathan pulled the rope hanging from the rafters. The rope, tied to the ores positioned between the rafters, triggered the fishing nets to fall onto the soldiers as they entered the hut. Nathan then turned and kicked the boards that were marked in red. The loosely attached boards fell, and an escape opened for the trapped couple. Nathan grabbed Esther's hand and led her out as the soldiers struggled on the floor of the hut.

"Run downhill toward the shoreline," he whispered. "Hide there until you hear my voice." Esther began running and Nathan drew his knife. The soldiers were not prepared to fight in such cramped quarters. Their swords were too long and their shields too bulky. As the first soldier exited the hut in the back, Nathan cut his throat and pulled him on out. The second soldier was still sprawled on his back under the net. Nathan looked down at him, and with some pity stepped on his sword and slit his throat too.

Nathan ran down the hill calling Esther's name as loudly as he dared. As he approached the shoreline, she responded from behind a large rock. Nathan grabbed her hand and led her to a ravine nearby. They huddled there for what seemed like an eternity afraid to breathe.

In about ten-minutes, the boat with Jonah, Enoch and Samuel quietly sailed to a small inlet near the ravine. They let down their nets and began holding the net while wading toward the shore, the usual way of fishing the ravine. Then Nathan told Esther, "You must enter the water and wade to the men. They will lift you into the boat and we will be off. Now go!" Without hesitation, Esther ran into the shallow water and into the arms of Jonah. He lifted her up quickly, turned and practically dumped her into the boat. Then as Nathan ran toward the boat, Samuel and Jonah threw the nets into the boat, and dove over the side into the boat too.

"Under the nets, Esther," Nathan ordered. Then they opened the sail as Nathan boarded the boat and drifted south across the lake far from shore.

Esther remained low, shivering inside the boat while Nathan and his crew appeared to be simple fishermen going about their business and drifting south. The commotion on the shore near Lamech's house distracted most observers.

Enoch quietly sank into shock. Esther raised her head to glare at him while Nathan pretended to fish. Nathan's crew straightened the nets, dumped the fish and tacked toward the south without speaking a word. They had no idea what they would do next.

Archelaus, ruled Samaria, Judea and Idumea. However, he could not rule. He was an embarrassment to Rome and destined to be replaced, but by whom?

Chapter 10

Every morning, Thomas taught Simeon scripture. Now Simeon understood why Thomas could talk directly to Yahweh, and he respected Thomas as a rabbi. He never dreamed he would have his own rabbi to teach him scripture and its meaning. He also understood that Thomas saw things a little differently than the others, but after talking to Irad and Seth he realized that Thomas was dear to most of those in Jerusalem and his teachings were considered well thought-out.

After one of the sessions, they had a little time before sunrise and Simeon asked some serious questions. "Why has the Messiah not come yet, Thomas?"

"I don't know, except to say his *time* has not come. You know, it is not for us to decide."

"Yes, but how will he come and how will we know him?"

"That is a little confusing even to me, Simeon. You see, the scriptures call him Wonderful, Counselor, Prince of Peace, and yet, he will be pieced and killed. I don't know if a sword or what will kill him, but I would like to think we'd know him, or we wouldn't call him those wonderful things. To some, he will be a capstone of their faith and yet to unbelievers he will be a rock on which to stumble. I would love to see the Messiah come!"

"I want the Messiah to come too, Thomas. The Romans killed my brother and my father. I hate the Romans and want the Messiah to kill them all or whatever he does to those who persecute his 'chosen people'."

"Well, there you may be surprised. He will come to save the world. I believe the 'world' means *the entire* world and not just us Jews. Remember, Yahweh promised Abraham that his offspring would be a blessing to *all* the nations? Perhaps he will make proselytes of the whole world, even those who are gentiles like the Romans. Then they will be our brothers and we will not have to fear them. What do you think, Simeon?"

"No wonder you got kicked out of the Temple! What do *I* think? You are the rabbi. I have no idea!"

"You need to learn to figure things out for yourself, Simeon. You won't always have a rabbi around to answer your questions. Besides, we rabbis aren't that smart ourselves."

"Don't tell me that, Thomas. I think you are the wisest man I have ever met, and others think so too." "Thank you, Simeon, but one piece of advice; don't hate so much. It isn't healthy."

Simeon and Thomas went inside and began to carry out some of the pottery for sale that morning. For the first time, Simeon had a few of his best pieces for display. They were unusual pieces and obviously not Thomas' work, but they were good, of course, or Thomas would not have put them out. Something about the sharp edges and crisp lines made them different from anything around, and it was as if they had a mind of their own, just like Simeon.

As the day progressed, it began to rain. Just then, a "regular" came to the shop and stood in the rain and picked-up Simeon's best piece, a pitcher. The man looked at Thomas and asked, "What is this?"

Thomas replied, "A pitcher."

Simeon held his breath wondering if the man would like it or say it was shoddy work.

"Did you make this, Thomas?"

"No," Thomas replied.

"Well, who did then?"

"Do you like it?" questioned Thomas with slight tilt of the head.

"I like it very much! I am thinking of buying it for my daughter. She is getting married soon, and I want something unusual to give her. This is special. I have seen nothing quite like it."

"There isn't any other like it in the world," said Thomas. For anyone else, it would cost plenty, but for you a *special* price."

The "regular" laughed and paid the special price. Then he squinted and looked Thomas straight in the eye. "Now, Thomas, who made this?"

Thomas smiled and said, "My student, Simeon, Son of Jacob from Bethlehem. Do you like his work?"

"Certainly, I bought it didn't I?" The man left with a smile on his face, holding the pitcher under his arm.

Simeon was ecstatic! He stood, spread his feet apart, put his hands on his hips and looked Thomas in the eye. Thomas praised him, and Simeon took it in like a sponge. Praise from Thomas meant everything to Simeon.

Finally, Thomas had the kind of son every man wanted, one who respects him and follows in his footsteps. Thomas knew Simeon would be a great potter someday.

Simeon could not wait to tell Rachel that he sold his first piece. That evening after dinner, Simeon and Rachel actually talked outside the shop. Although Thomas and Rachel's parents noticed, they didn't seem to mind the two talking and just observed, with interest, as they feigned not noticing. Simeon excitedly told of the man buying the pitcher as a gift for his daughter while gesturing with animation never seen by Thomas or the others. Rachel listened with a smile and shared his joy but said little or nothing.

While Simeon carried on, Rachel looked Simeon in the eyes with new appreciation. She gazed into his dark, brown eyes and felt something she had never felt before. It was a feeling of excitement and closeness, a feeling of wanting to be with him all evening, talking of all sorts of things. She felt as if she had discovered something new that had been there all along. Simeon was not like the other boys she had seen about the town. He was special to her, and she felt special with him. Then her heart beat faster, and she broke the gaze. After saying something to express her joy at Simeon's success, she began to wonder if he could accept a "half-breed."

He became quiet and as he walked back into the shop, and he wondered if she was spoken for. He could ask Thomas about her but decided that even Thomas had no way of knowing and dropped the thought.

Thomas had watched them talking outside the shop in silence and wondered if something was wrong, but decided it was just the opposite when Simeon smiled as he passed Thomas and entered the small living quarters. Thomas decided the problem was that something was very *right*.

The next morning, Simeon put out more of his own pieces. Only a few sold, but it pleased him. Even Thomas didn't sell every piece. Simeon decided he would make more pitchers and urns and concentrate on them for a while. He didn't think there was much he could do with a bowl. Simeon also decided he would work hard to be, truly, the greatest potter in all of Judea.

Thomas was pleased too. He knew he was running out of time, and if Simeon could sell his products now, then surely by the end of Thomas' life, Simeon would be a master potter. More importantly, Simeon would be a good man, gentle in heart, generous to a fault and know the scriptures.

Jared was not blind either. After he thought Rachel was asleep, he asked Aiko, "What does Rachel think of Simeon? He is an out-of-town boy after all, but he is learning a trade very quickly and has the best rabbi of all for a teacher."

Aiko just smiled and said, "I think Simeon is a good boy. What do you think?"

Jared smiled, "He reminds me of myself when I met you, all eyes and no brains."

Aiko just laughed and said, "I sense the same thing. He is a lot like you. Rachel always tries to look her best when Simeon is around, and I think she likes him, but she never says so to me. What do you think we should do?"

"Let me talk to Thomas and see what he thinks. Do you think he would approve?"

"Of course he would, Jared, he married us against everyone else's judgment. Thomas does not care if Rachel is a full-blooded Jew or not, as long as she is a believer. What about Simeon's mother? She should have something to say. Do you agree?"

"He is Thomas' responsibility. How could she know if Rachel is a good choice for her son?" Jared said with his characteristic finality.

With that, Aiko retreated inside to get ready for bed. Rachel just lay there with her eyes closed on her mat wondering what her parents would do. She was afraid of being betrothed, but if Simeon was the choice, it was acceptable to her. She would wait for one of her parents to ask though because it was the right thing to do. That night Rachel dreamed of being the wife of a potter.

Nearly a year passed, and Rachel and Simeon saw more of each other every day. Finally, Jared approached Thomas and asked if Rachel might be a good match for Simeon. Usually mothers did such work, so it was a little awkward since Thomas was in charge of Simeon.

Before the conversation was over, Jared and Thomas were laughing at themselves and the situation, two grown men stumbling over such a topic.

Simeon didn't have much to offer for a bride, but Jared saw no reason to demand much since he didn't need much and thought Rachel would be happy with the choice. So now, Jared and Thomas had to approach their children with the proposition of marriage.

Simeon was outside talking to a "regular" when Thomas and Irad came outside. Thomas said he needed to talk to Simeon about something important and that Irad could watch the shop. Both Simeon and Thomas went inside with Seth, and then Thomas sent Seth out to fetch some more firewood for the kiln, a time-consuming job.

Placing his hand on Simeon's shoulder and with a sober look on his face, Thomas began, "I want to talk to you about your future, Simeon. Some day you need to marry a good woman and settle down."

Simeon almost laughed, wondering how he could be more "settled down" than this.

Thomas went on, "Rachel is a fine girl, and she has wonderful parents. I have talked to Jared, and we think she may be a good match for you. I think we should act now before someone else comes along and steals her from us. Do you think she is as wonderful as I do?"

Simeon's eyes grew large, and he stiffened. He liked Rachel, but it was a little scary to think of spending his whole life with her. Yet, he could not argue that she was certainly his favorite of all the people he had met, and now he had a trade and wanted to make something great of his life. "Yes, Thomas, I think she is wonderful too. Do we need to do this now?"

"Yes, Simeon, I think so. She grows more beautiful every day, and the more she is out in front of the shop, the more people notice her. Jared wants her to have a good man, like you, who likes her and will take care of her. It is serious for him and Aiko! She is their only daughter, and it is a wonderful honor for them to offer her to you. They must think very highly of you, my son."

Simeon flinched. Thomas had referred to Simeon as "son" but it seemed so natural. Thomas cared for Simeon like a father, and he knew Thomas loved him so how could he say no.

"I agree, Thomas. You are right, as usual. I like Rachel very much, and I would hate to marry somebody I don't know. She is great, and so is her family."

With that, Thomas hugged Simeon and lifted his feet from the floor with his strong arms, just as Seth came in with the firewood.

"Well, what have we here, a celebration?" asked Seth.

"Yes, Seth we're having a great celebration. Simeon, here, has agreed to be betrothed to the most beautiful young woman in all of Jerusalem!"

Seth joked, "But my wife is married already! Oh, but you said a *young* woman. That must be Rachel!"

Simeon laughed and Irad bellowed from outside, "Hey, keep it down in there! We have business to conduct out here!"

Irad came in and then he and Seth hugged Simeon too. They all laughed and began telling stories about their own betrothal.

"I had never seen my wife before I married her. She was beautiful to me though. It took us quite a while to get to where we could talk intelligently to each other and still, I don't understand her sometimes!" Seth offered.

They laughed and agreed that neither of them understands his wife much.

Thomas was quiet. He smiled and laughed with them, but he said nothing of his deceased wife, Naomi. His eyes had a faraway look, and a small almost indiscernible tear filled his eye. Simeon noticed, but Irad and Seth continued to joke with each other about their wives….sometimes not very politely. Finally, a customer put an end to their fun, and they all went back to work, except Thomas who hung his head and started toward Jared's house.

Jared was out doing his business of trading, but Aiko was there and looked at Thomas anxiously. She waited for Thomas to speak first.

"Is Rachel around?" he asked.

"No," Aiko replied.

"Good. I talked to Simeon, and he is honored to accept the betrothal. I believe he thinks, as I do, that Rachel is a wonderful girl and would make a wonderful wife."

It was Aiko's turn to cry, but she cried openly. "Oh, Thomas, what a gift you have in Simeon. I talked to Rachel just last night, and she *adores* him. She said she was sorry that she was not truly kind to him when he first appeared, but she has grown to love the way he shares with her like no one else. I believe they are perfect for each other, Thomas!"

Thomas wanted to hug Aiko but knew better. He stumbled for words but succeeded to bid her a good day and backed out of the room as she sat there on a bench crying her heart out. He turned, and there stood Rachel! He stumbled into her and she laughed, "Do you always back out of doors, Thomas?"

Thomas looked at Rachel. *Just what the boy needs. She loves him and has the sense of humor to get her through the hard times. She has spunk.*

"No, Rachel, just when the host is bawling her eyes out."

Rachel looked alarmed and stepped inside the doorway. She looked at her mother and immediately thought something bad had happened to Jared. "What is wrong, Mother?" she asked.

Aiko just opened her arms and said, "Nothing dear. Come hug your mother."

Aiko and Rachel talked all afternoon about the betrothal. Her mother told of her marriage with Jared and how difficult it was at first since she was a proselyte. They cried together, laughed together and then cried some more, until Jared came home.

He entered the room and said, "I see you received an answer from Thomas, but I can't tell if it is good or bad." He didn't understand women most of the time either.

"It is a wonderful answer, Father," said Rachel, as she rushed to her tall, strong, but gentle father. "I love him, and I believe he loves me too!"

"I guess that means the betrothal is on?"

"Of course," Aiko responded.

"Good. What's for supper?" asked Jared.

The women laughed, for some reason unknown to Jared, and began fixing dinner.

While they were busy with dinner, Jared walked over to the pottery shop, peeked in at Thomas and gave him thumbs-up and a wink. Thomas returned the thumbs-up and smiled. Then Jared turned and headed back home with a satisfied smile on his face. His daughter had made a good catch, and he had a good, responsible son-in-law. A year later, they would be married.

Herod Antipas could tolerate no more outbursts from the local Jews for fear of appearing weak like his brother. Something had to be done.

Chapter 11

The next year was wonderful for Simeon and Rachel. They walked up the hill together and even sat in the olive garden on the other side of the Kidron Valley making plans for the future. Rachel introduced Simeon to her life-long friends in Jerusalem, some of which were also betrothed.

Simeon continued with his pottery making, and soon Thomas decided that Simeon needed a mark for his work. Simeon chose two almonds as his mark. Thomas approved and immediately understood why Simeon chose such a mark. From that day on, every piece in the shop bore the scorpion mark of Thomas or the almond eyes of Simeon, two master-potters. The regulars noticed Rachel was outside the shop nearly every day.

Irad and Seth worked closely with Simeon and showed no jealousy or resentment of his success. They even helped

Simeon build an addition onto the shop for him and Rachel to use after the marriage. Simeon tried every possible way to make his pottery better, and finally he asked Thomas about the vase in Aiko's home. Thomas truly did not know how to make such a piece. The white clay was definitely different, and the bright paint with the golden outline on the surface was definitely something he could not duplicate.

It frustrated Simeon that there was someone in the world making better pottery than he made. It was not enough to be the best in Jerusalem.

One hot, summer day, a camel passed the shop with a jar much like Aiko's vase. Simeon jumped up in a near panic, and as the wheel slowly ground to a halt, his piece flopped onto the ground. He rushed to the camel, knocking some finished pieces to the hard pavement and begged the driver to stop. "I must see your wares!" shouted Simeon.

"Then come to the market," the man responded in a strange dialect and rode on.

Early that evening, Rachel and Simeon set out for the marketplace hoping to find the merchant. After traveling down a few streets, they found the strangely dressed man sitting on a colorful blanket drinking wine from a cup made by Thomas, oddly enough.

Simeon began, "I'm the man who asked about your wares on the street going up the hill, back there. I am most interested in knowing where you found this jar."

"These are made far to the East, but I bought it from a merchant in Alexandria. You can buy more there or buy this one at a special price."

Simeon figured a "special price" would be far more than he had.

In despair, Simeon asked, "What special price do you have in mind?"

"The girl," he replied, quite matter-of-factly.

Simeon was horrified! He wished he had gone alone. He backed away and looked around to be sure others were not surrounding them. Rachel hung onto his arm, petrified at the thought.

"Let's get out of here, Rachel," Simeon whispered.

He never answered the merchant. Simeon and Rachel rushed down the hill to their homes, and when they returned to Rachel's house, they stood for a moment, out of breath. Rachel cried so hard that she could hardly talk.

"Rachel, there is no way I would do that! I love you. I want you to know that. There is nothing more valuable to me than you."

Rachel answered, still sobbing. "I love you too, Simeon. We will do well together."

She reached up to Simeon's face and stroked his cheek, then went inside.

That same night, Simeon shared the story of the jar and the merchant with Thomas. Simeon explained that he wanted to inspect the jar and possibly break it open to analyze the clay and the paint.

Thomas understood the curiosity about the jar, but said to Simeon, "Be careful, my boy, where you take Rachel. There are those who would just take her! You may have been very blessed by the offer and not the taking."

Simeon felt very ashamed of himself. Jared and Aiko had trusted them to walk together and now he had put her in danger. His anger at the merchant grew each time he thought about it.

Chapter 12

Nathan told Samuel and Jonah, "We need to split-up. I will let you off at Magdala. You travel southward by the main highway, and then we can meet outside Tiberius, sell the boat, and take the road east of Mount Tabor. We will meet where the highways intersect south of Nazareth. Wait for us there. Hurry, you can swim to shore from here."

Samuel and Jonah dived out of the boat just offshore of Magdala. It was not unusual for fishermen to swim a few meters to disembark there. Nathan, Enoch and Esther sailed on to Tiberius.

Romans were everywhere in Tiberius, but it was too early for Marcus to get a message there even by horseback. Nathan pulled his boat up to shore near town just as a man approached.

"You and your family can't leave your boat here! Who do you think you are?"

Nathan smiled his best smile. "I and my family need to sell this boat. If this is your land, we will either sell the boat to you at a bargain or give you part of the proceeds if you will let us sell it from here. What do you say? It is a good opportunity!"

Seeing a good chance to make quick money, the landowner smiled also. "And what do you want for this wreck of a fishing boat?"

"It's really a fine boat. I have everything fishermen need to get started. Do you know of a young fisherman ready to start his own business?" Nathan did not want to sell to this greedy man.

"I have a nephew who is out fishing now. What do you want for the boat?"

Resigned to a poor bargain, Nathan replied, "What seems fair to you?"

"Four-hundred Drachmas," the man replied. He evidently didn't know much about boats because the boat was actually worth much less.

"Well, I hate to take such a small amount. I'll only take it if you have the coins now. My family needs to move to Cana."

"You have a deal, my friend!"

The man paid Nathan, and the two of them pulled the boat unceremoniously up onto the tall, slick grass.

"Thank you, kind sir, do you know where we can catch the road to Cana?" asked Nathan.

Enoch and Esther stood stark still on shore, afraid to talk. They knew that Cana was not their destination but were amazed at Nathan's cunning. They left the town going north, stopped at a shop, bought some blankets for the trip and then circled around town to the south. When evening came, they took the main road out of town along the edge of the sea.

About ten kilometers south of town, they bedded down for the night. All three slept close together with Esther in the middle, between Enoch, her son, and Nathan, her protector. Enoch and Esther dreamed of running from soldiers. Nathan didn't sleep.

The next day around sundown, the three joined Samuel and Jonah at the intersection of the highways.

"Samuel! Jonah! Are you alright?"

"Yes, Nathan, but we're cold, hungry and tired. We were afraid to ask for food for fear of the Romans. Are you okay?"

"We're fine. Here is most of the money I received for the boat. We bought blankets and some bread for you too."

"Do you think the Romans have any idea where we are?" asked Samuel with a mouthful of bread.

"No, but we cannot travel together. Where do you want to go, Samuel?"

"Jonah and I want to get back to fishing. we're going to the Great Sea somewhere. Do you have a suggestion?"

"Try to get work in Caesarea. There are plenty of jobs there, and you can mingle with plenty of people. You may want to split-up, at least for a time."

"Where are you going?"

"I don't know yet, but we will head south. Shalom brothers!" Nathan embraced his friends with a tenderness that surprised Esther. Enoch sensed family in a way that he had not felt since that night in Bethlehem.

The two crewmembers headed west, while the others began the long trek to Alexandria and safety.

Chapter 13

Simeon had a burning desire to get to Alexandria and search for an Eastern vase. He wondered how he could leave the shop, Thomas, and Rachel to get to Alexandria and back before the wedding. He simply had to have a piece of that pottery to cut and analyze, so he too could make such a white piece with bright decoration.

Finally, Thomas noticed the distress of Simeon and asked, "What is wrong with you, my boy? You seem to have your mind elsewhere."

Simeon replied, "I am haunted by the vase. Every time I look at it, I want to smash it to pieces, scrape the outside surface and analyze the ingredients. I wonder how the potter made the gold and brightly colored paint stay on the outside without cracking the clay. I need answers!"

"You are really jealous of these other craftsmen, aren't you? If you go by boat, I guess you can get to Alexandria and back before the wedding. The question is; can you find a piece like you want in Alexandria?"

"I don't feel like I can leave Rachel, you and the others to go wandering around Alexandria looking for a piece of pottery."

"Go, Simeon. We will be fine, and you can satisfy your curiosity one way or another. Leave soon, and don't frustrate yourself further."

"I must talk to Rachel first."

"Fine, but don't delay."

Simeon finished the day and took the evening walk with Rachel. She had noticed the uneasiness of Simeon also, but dared not ask for fear he was bothered by the wedding.

Finally, Simeon began. "Rachel, Thomas has offered to let me go to Alexandria to search for a piece like the merchant had in the market. I feel like I need to understand the process and find the clay, so I can be the best potter possible. If I don't learn, someone else will, and I will be out of business."

"I understand, Simeon, but I want to go with you and can't until we're married. Can you wait until after the wedding? Then I can go with you?"

"I don't think I should wait. We had a frightening experience with the merchant here, and they probably are worse there. I need to go now *before* we're married. But I am not sure that I have the time."

"Then you must go now and not wait any longer," Rachel said. "I will be here for you when you get back. Thomas and my parents will take fine care of me. I want you to be happy, Simeon."

"I will search for a boat on the Great Sea tomorrow. Perhaps I can find a boat to Alexandria that leaves soon enough. If I can't find something in Alexandria in four days, I'll return. Is that acceptable to you?"

"Yes, my love. I will see you off in the morning."

They walked and talked more about their dreams and plans for the future. Rachel also wanted Simeon to be the best potter in the world. She sincerely shared his dream.

The next day, Simeon climbed the hill, looking for Jews who had made the pilgrimage from Egypt to Jerusalem. He entered the outer court of the temple and found a friend of Rachel, a young Levi priest named Nadab.

"Do you remember me Nadab? I am Simeon, Son of Jacob from Bethlehem, betrothed to Rachel.

"Of course, I remember you, Simeon. How are you and what brings you here looking for me? You don't have cold feet do you?"

"No, of course not. I am looking for a group headed for Alexandria, or somewhere beyond Alexandria, to travel with. Do you know of such a group?"

"No, but I am sure someone in here knows. Why do you want to go to Alexandria, Simeon? It is a long way off, and so close to the wedding."

"You know that I am a potter with Thomas' shop. I have discovered a source for a special kind of pottery that can only be found in Alexandria. I need to find a piece to analyze and learn how they make this special pottery. It is beautiful."

"I know exactly what you mean! It is the vase that belongs to Aiko isn't it? It is beautiful. You know, I have always wanted to go to Alexandria myself. I wish I could go along. Come with me, and we will ask around to see if my fellow priests or scribes know of a caravan."

The two made friends immediately, and Nadab quickly found an excursion to Alexandria for Simeon, leaving in three days. In return, Simeon invited Nadab home with him to dinner, and hoped that Rachel or her mother would fix something for the two of them.

Rachel was pleased to see Simeon and Nadab together. She liked Nadab and knew he could be trusted more than most others in the temple. She and Aiko fixed a fine meal and invited Thomas too. The six of them shared a good evening together after Jared came home.

Jared was interested in the adventure too and said, "I was surprised that you could find a caravan so quickly. Why not travel together? You have always wanted to go to Alexandria, Nadab. Can you get some time off to go to Alexandria? The trip would be educational at least and exciting at best."

"Oh, I don't know if they would let me go, but I sure would like to go with Simeon. I think I *will* ask. I can probably find some good reason to go," Nadab reasoned. "This vase would look beautiful in the temple. We have so little pottery in our quarters where we stay. Now, I *really* want to go with you. Perhaps I can! The temple *needs* something like this."

"When you ask the Chief Priest, tell him I would keep an eye on you," suggested Simeon.

"Yea right!" laughed Nadab, "After dinner, can you come with me, Simeon, and bring the vase?"

"No problem."

Women are not allowed in special parts of the temple and certainly cannot go into the area of the Chief Priest. Rachael knew she couldn't go with the men. She cleaned the table as the men reclined and discussed politics and religion. She resented the way men left their wives out of the men's business.

Two days later, it was time to leave. Rachel and Simeon lingered alone for a short while inside to say their goodbye's, and Simeon had the opportunity to pledge his love to her. She in turn reminded him to be careful and to keep Nadab with him at all times for safety.

"I will be here when you return," Rachel assured him.

Simeon met Nadab at the edge of town, and they began their trip with the Egyptian Jews. They were an interesting bunch, but not actually friendly, so Nadab and Simeon traveled as a distant attachment to the caravan.

In Caesarea, they saw the big wooden ships that traveled the Great Sea. More than a few headed for Alexandria, and theirs was one of the largest. It sat stately in the water but was obviously loaded since the sea came well up on the hull. The crew and dockworkers were busy loading some last miscellaneous cargo and hustled to finish in time to catch the tide. Both Simeon and Nathan knew enough about sailing that it would be a smooth trip by comparison to sailing on smaller boats and were excited to see the grand vessel.

At last, they disembarked from Caesarea with a crew of nearly three hundred. It was an exciting experience to watch the wind fill the sails and the ship leap as it caught the wind. The masts creaked and groaned until the speed of the ship more or less matched the speed of the wind and things settled down. There was never rest for the crew as they shifted the sails at the command of the captain. It was a hectic deck.

The sound of the ship cutting through the water was soothing, however, and comforting to Simeon. The ship and the sea were beautiful to him as he considered how wonderful it would be to become a world traveler. Simeon felt like he had conquered the sea itself. His father would have been thrilled to take such a trip. He was thankful to Thomas for paying the price for him to go.

Nadab stood on the deck with his head hung over the side and an ashen color to his face. He was not having much fun. His stomach definitely didn't like the sea or any part of it, and he saw little beauty in such a mode of travel. He felt more like the sea had conquered him.

The majestic ship went straight to Alexandria without stopping, although most ships stopped at various ports along the way for trade. However, this was an Egyptian cargo vessel and headed for home loaded with merchandise.

A crewmember told the passengers about the Pharos that would show its light the final morning of the journey. Simeon woke before sunrise to see the magnificent light on the horizon. It shimmered across the calm sea with a golden glow that resembled the canola fields back home. It must have been nearly twenty kilometers away when they first saw the famous lighthouse on the island. Simeon had heard of the wonder before and found it more exciting to behold than he had imagined. Nothing in all of Judea was so tall or stately. They sailed on to sunrise, and the night fire of the Pharos turned into a blazing reflection of the sun as they entered the port.

Simeon and Nadab disembarked, and signed the paper stating that they had been on board and were leaving the ship. The Egyptians were sticklers for record keeping since Alexander the Macedonian had destroyed their library and much of their history was lost. Now they wrote everything down as if it would make up for their loss somehow.

"Remember, Nadab, I have only four days to locate the pottery. We must hurry and visit all the markets we can."

They searched that first day without any results, and that evening they checked into a small, dingy inn and then searched for some food. The streets of Alexandria were darker than the streets of Jerusalem. Simeon and Nadab surveyed the buildings and the people. More than language was different here, and one could sense tension in the air as vendors sat on the street with wares that neither Jew had seen before. Odd carvings of grotesque animals set among burning incense, foreign currency exchanges and Egyptian cosmetics signaled unfamiliar cultures coming together in a patchwork of sights and smells.

Simeon was relieved that Rachel was not with him. It was frightening to Simeon, and at times, his heart beat faster just out of fright at what he saw. He could not abide this place for long.

That night Simeon slept restlessly. He dreamed of dark streets and painted people.

Archelaus was such an embarrassment to Rome that they removed him from power and replaced him with Pontius Pilate. Pilate was a worthy choice. He could control the Jewish leadership by compromise where compromise cost Rome nothing.

Chapter 14

Nathan, Esther and Enoch arrived in Alexandria with a sizable sum in their pockets from the sale of the boat. To keep their cover, Nathan and Esther let folks assume they were married and Enoch's parents. Their first order of business was to find a place to stay. They located a small inn suitable for travelers since it provided meals and some extras. This would do until they found a better place.

Nathan and Enoch walked down to the shore the next day and looked over the fishing vessels there on the Great Sea. Enoch had heard of the boats of the Great Sea but had never seen one. They were much more complex and larger than Enoch had imagined. Working on such boats would be like learning to fish all over again. The sea seemed large and foreboding, going to the edge of the earth.

Nathan, of course, had been to the Great Sea and was less intimidated. He walked up to a small group of sailors and asked where to find work. They pointed north and gave directions to the docks where fishermen lined-up and were hired by the day. The western accent of the fishermen was strange to Enoch, and he didn't like them just because of their accent. Nathan was unaffected.

Back at the inn, Esther arranged their few belongings and proceeded to the dining room. It was an upper room and small for the number of guests. The tables were tall and hard, uncomfortable benches were along the sides of the tables. In a similar custom to Judean inns, the women ate separately, allowing them a chance to talk freely but, more importantly, letting the men talk without their wives.

After Esther seated herself, the woman who sat next to Esther asked, "Where are you from?"

Esther froze and wondered what to say. She knew that if she answered that she was from somewhere far from Bethlehem, her accent would reveal her as a liar. "From southern Judea," she responded, purposely not mentioning a specific town.

"I am Sarah. My husband and I are from Jerusalem where he had a small metal shop. He plans to start one up here to specialize in ship tackle. Why are you here?"

Esther really wanted to avoid these questions, but Sarah seemed kind and relaxed, so Esther trusted her and remained engaged in conversation. "I have a son with us here in Alexandria that wants to fish the Great Sea. He will do fine, I am sure."

"Well, Alexandria seems like a good place to find work and learn the trade," responded Sarah. "We begin our work tomorrow. May I see you at breakfast?"

Esther agreed and with that, Sarah decided to ask no more questions since Esther seemed a little disturbed by her questions. Sarah just nodded goodbye.

Chapter 15

Simeon and Nadab rose early for breakfast and joined the other men in their dining area. After reconnoitering the room, they reclined near the door with their backs to the wall so they could view the array of men in the small room.

There, facing them on the other wall, sat Enoch and Nathan. Simeon squinted hard at his brother, unsure of what he saw. Years had passed, and his handsome, older brother had grown to full height and gained weight. After making sure of what he saw, he said to Nadab, "I need to go talk to a man across the room. I believe I know him. Do you mind?"

"No, that's fine," replied Nadab, with his mouth full. "But be careful what you say."

Slowly, Simeon rose to his feet, walked around those nearby and started across the room. His heart began to beat faster, as he weaved in and out amongst the closely situated patrons. Finally, he stood across from his brother. Nathan looked up first and moved his hand to the dagger in his belt. Then Enoch looked up and the brothers' eyes met.

Simeon broke the silence. "Are you Enoch, Son of Jacob from Bethlehem?"

"Simeon! I thought that was you. Why are you here in Alexandria? I thought you were in Jerusalem with the potter!"

"I could ask the same, brother," replied Simeon. "I am looking for a special kind of pottery to possibly make in our shop. And you?"

There was a long pause. Enoch didn't know what to say. He was tempted to tell the whole truth for he was not accustomed to lying to his little brother or making up some story of adventure. "I am traveling with Nathan here," glancing at his companion, "and our mother." There was no way he would speak of the run-in with the Romans here among so many.

"You mean Mother is here somewhere too?"

"Yes, I think she is outside right now looking at the flowers in the court. She has apparently made friends with a woman from Jerusalem."

"I must see Mother! Come with me Enoch. We can have breakfast anytime."

Enoch excused himself from Nathan who relaxed since Enoch had spoken often of his younger brother. Then Enoch and Simeon rushed down the stairway and out the door, stumbling over each other on the way.

"Mother," Simeon shouted.

Esther turned slowly. Her tired eyes lit with the beauty and radiance of a youthful mother as she anticipated the sight of her young son. Simeon ran to her and embraced her as he used to do as a youth. Time seemed to reverse itself, and the family that struggled so much in Bethlehem after that night was together again for a wonderful moment.

"Simeon! Oh, how you have grown! Let me look at you."

Simeon backed away and glanced at Enoch. Then he turned back to his mother. She was gazing at him with a smile on her lips and a sigh in her heart. Esther could hardly contain her joy.

"My boys are together with me again! Oh, how I am blessed! You are such handsome young men. Walk with me here in the garden, and tell me about your life as a potter, Simeon."

"There really isn't much to tell about the work, except that I am good at it, and Thomas is a wonderful teacher.

He even teaches me scripture! He used to be a rabbi in the Temple. However, the real news is that I am betrothed to a wonderful girl. Her name is Rachel."

"Rachel is a beautiful name. Is she with you, Simeon?"

"No, Mother, she is back at the pottery shop with her mother and father and Thomas. I'm only here for a few days. What occasion brings you here?"

Trapped by his son's questions, Esther frowned. What could she say?

"It is not all good news, Simeon," replied Esther. "Lamech, your uncle, is dead along with your cousins and their mother. The Romans slaughtered them in their own home. Nathan saved both of us. It was *awful*!" She lowered her head and looked at the ground, her eyes growing tired again.

Enoch broke the silence this time. "We're safe here in Alexandria, Simeon. There is no need to worry. But we cannot return to Jerusalem, Galilee or Bethlehem or they will surely find us and kill us too."

"Why? Why do the Romans want to kill you?"

"Lamech was a Zealot, Simeon. He and his fellow fishermen wanted to kill Romans more than they wanted to fish," explained Enoch. "Nathan saved us just in time. He is not a Zealot, but the Romans think he is. It's a mess, Simeon."

"Oh! I thought you were both safe in Galilee, and you, Enoch, were learning a trade."

"I was, Simeon. Nathan taught me to fish, and now we are going to fish the Great Sea and make our living here. It will be difficult, but our hope is here. There is no future for us in Galilee."

"Can I help in any way?"

"Yes," replied Enoch. "Keep our secret from the man traveling with you, and don't tip our hand. You must stay away from us for your own good. we're like lepers to you! Have nothing to do with us!"

"How can I do that, Enoch? This is my mother!"

"It is for your Mother's sake!"

Simeon looked at his mother and Enoch. He had often wondered if he would ever see them again but planned to visit them in Galilee to introduce his new bride. Now he felt, again, that he was without a family. Tears began to form in his eyes. He stood there a moment and then hurried to his mother and held her in his arms.

Simeon backed away and turned to Enoch, "I understand. I won't ever mention your being in Alexandria. Your secret is safe with me. I love you both and give my regards to Nathan. I am not going up. Nadab, my friend, will come out, and I'll tell him that I became ill and needed fresh air. He will buy my story.

May Yahweh protect you?" He turned, and walked to the front of the inn, sat down on a stone bench, held his head in his trembling hands and wept.

Enoch and Esther stayed in the garden. Only one person heard the conversation. Sarah heard their words but seemed to understand that some things require keeping in the heart.

Nadab came down to find a pale Simeon sitting on the bench looking like death itself. "What is the matter, Simeon? You look awful."

"Oh, I just felt hot, and my stomach became upset. The fresh air has made me feel better."

"You call this stink fresh air! Boy, you *are* sick! Come. Let's find the pottery we so eagerly seek and get out of here. Was the person someone you knew? I saw you leave with him in a hurry."

"He was just an old friend from Bethlehem. His mother was here, and I wanted to see her too, before they left. They're gone now." Simeon's heart grieved at the thought of never seeing them again.

Simeon and Nadab headed for the marketplace. Alexandria was a much larger town than they had imagined, the streets were very dark and, of course, the Egyptians seemed very strange to Simeon and Nadab. Since the streets were long, it took all day to cover just a few. Nadab was a big help by going down one side of the street and Simeon the other. Language was somewhat of a barrier, but they got the hang of it quickly.

Finally, on the third day, Nadab and Simeon were passing down a little-traveled market street. The street merchants were more like beggars than businessmen, but Nadab noticed pottery on a blanket by an older man with weathered skin. "Do you have any pottery with brightly colored decoration?" He asked.

The man pulled a vase from a cloth bag and placed it upright before Nadab. Nadab gasped! It was the real thing as far as he could tell. "Simeon! Come here! Come Here! I think I have found one!"

Simeon excused himself from the poor merchant he was talking to and crossed the street quickly, bumping a few people along the way. "What have you found, Nadab?"

Then he saw it! The vase was nearly the same size as the one Aiko had brought from her homeland. It was brightly decorated and just as attractive as the one on Aiko's shelf. It was white and decorated in many colors. Simeon reached for it, but the man stopped his hand. "Not so quick, young man. Do you aim to rob me, an old man?"

"Of course not! I am sorry, sir. My name is Simeon, Son of Jacob from Bethlehem in Judea. I am in Alexandria looking for a certain type of pottery, and it appears that this is what I am looking for. May I inspect it more closely?"

"I suppose," responded the man in a strange dialect. "This comes from the East."

Inspecting the vase, Simeon was convinced it was the same workmanship, or similar, to that of Aiko's vase. He admired it and inspected it inside and out. Then he realized he had botched any chance to bargain with the man. He turned to the merchant and respectfully asked, "How much are you asking for this vase?"

The merchant sighed. "I have carried this thing around for some time, and I need food. For you... a special price."

Always a special price! "Okay, how much," he asked.

The man looked Simeon in the eyes as if to study him. He debated going for a high price, but decided against it. He didn't have long to live anyway, and this young man appreciated the art of the vase. Perhaps it had found a home where it would receive the honor it was due. "I will take one-half Drachma."

Simeon was stunned. He expected to spend more than a day's wage for the vase. This was too good to believe. He asked, "Are you sure? We want to pay a fair price."

Nadab sighed at Simeon's poor bargaining skills.

The man replied, "It is yours, young man, bag and all."

With that, Simeon bought his prized possession. Now his only aim was to get home to Rachel and their wedding.

That night he and Nadab headed for the docks. They found a much smaller ship headed for ports along the Great Sea, so they left Alexandria early the next morning.

Simeon carried the vase himself, protecting it as if it were a child.

Priests came and went at the temple. Each had his personal, political agenda and strove for a higher place in the hierarchy. The Romans kept a close eye on the priests and allowed them only limited freedom to rule their own religious establishment. It was a tentative arrangement at best. Herod Antipas, the half-Jew, ruled the North, while Pilate, the Roman, ruled the South.

No love was lost between the two.

Chapter 16

Simeon and Nadab were excited to enter Jerusalem, and they went directly to the lower part of the city. Simeon, hunched down to avoid the cold and Rain. He beat on Thomas's door. Eventually Seth opened the door wide for them but said nothing. Simeon led Nadab inside, and they both shook the rain from their cloaks. Then Seth took their cloaks and hung them on a wooden peg protruding from one of the shelves. The two travelers plopped down by the small fire of the kiln, rubbing their hands together. Seth sat down with them, not going for Thomas.

"Did you find the piece?" asked Seth.

"Yes! I have it here. Want to see it?"

"Sure," Seth replied with only a hint of enthusiasm.

Simeon pulled it from under his shirt where he had kept it dry, as if water would somehow harm it. "Is Thomas asleep already? He is usually still up. Let's get him. He will be excited to see it." Simeon said as he rose.

Without looking up, Seth pulled on Simeon's sleeve to sit him down. There was no joy in Seth's face….no new riddles. He just sat there. Simeon and Nadab both sensed that something was seriously wrong.

"Thomas died while you were gone, Simeon. There was nothing any of us could do."

"What do you mean died? He was fine when I left. He was …fine," Simeon's broken voice trailed off.

Seth still stared at the floor and wrung his hands. "Thomas could not talk for a few minutes. Then he sat down, looked at us, closed his eyes, bent over and fell forward. I called to the others, and they came. He opened his eyes and looked at us all for a moment. His heart kept beating for a while as he struggled to communicate, but he never came around again. He just died. I am sorry, Simeon, we couldn't do anything."

"When did this happen?"

"It was only two days after you left. Rachel, Jared and Aiko helped us with Thomas' body, and arranged for his burial. We buried him in the cemetery on the way to the Mount of Olives. He always liked it so much there. Rachel sorted some of the pottery Thomas had finished. Irad and I dried it and fired it. Then Rachel worked hard to sell all we had. People asked for Thomas, and we had to tell them. They asked about you, and we said you would be back soon and the shop would continue. I hope that is true. It is, isn't it?"

"Of course, the shop will go on, Seth. we're a *family*. We always will be." The words were bittersweet to Simeon. He realized that indeed, this was his family, those he loved the most. He would never leave them.

Simeon turned to Nadab. "Can you help to make sure Thomas is honored properly at the temple? He was a great rabbi even if some of the others didn't agree with him."

"Yes, there are enough of his friends there to get that done. Not everyone felt he was a rebel, and many loved him greatly. I will take care of it for you. Now, go and see Rachel, Simeon. She must be eager to see you."

Simeon left the shop without his cloak or the precious piece of pottery.

Nadab rose slowly, lifted his cloak from the peg and followed a short distance behind Simeon. Nadab glanced at Simeon beating frantically on the neighboring door, then turned and started up the hill against the pelting rain.

Simeon was sobbing as he beat on the door. He wondered if Rachel would be glad to see him or angry because he had gone searching for the vase just when Thomas needed him most. He was furious with himself.

Jared came to the door. "Simeon! It is wonderful to have you back, my boy. Let me get Rachel, she will be so thrilled to see you." Simeon slipped inside out of the rain and softly closed the door behind him.

Hearing Simeon's voice, Rachel came from behind the curtain of her bedroom. She ran to Simeon with tears in her eyes and arms wide open. She nearly knocked Simeon over. "Oh Simeon, I have missed you so much. Have you heard about Thomas?"

"Yes, Seth told me just now. Nadab and I just got back."

"It was terrible, Simeon. He loved you so much, and I know he wanted to say something, but it just would not come out. His hands would not work right, so he could not leave you a message, but his eyes, oh his eyes... they spoke."

Simeon held Rachel close and spoke softly. "He was a father to me. He taught me so much. It will never be the same."

"Where is Nadab?"

"He must have gone, Rachel. He knew I would want to see you as soon as I could, and I guess he went back up the hill."

Realizing that Rachael and Simeon needed to talk, Jared and Aiko retreated to their room although they could obviously hear the slightest whisper in the small home.

"Rachel, I need to tell you something," Simeon began quietly. "I met my mother and brother in Alexandria. They were there hiding from the Romans while my brother fished the Great Sea."

"Why would Enoch and your mother hide from Romans, Simeon, and in Alexandria of all places?"

"It seems that my uncle was a Zealot in Galilee. Nathan, one of his fishermen, had no part of the Zealot thing and helped them escape my brother's home, just as the Romans attacked. My uncle and his family are dead, and now Enoch and Nathan fish the Great Sea in order to make a living. It's bizarre. I may never see them again, Rachel. Now Thomas is gone. It's such a relief to see you are well and have waited for me. I feel foolish that I left for such a selfish reason. Nevertheless, if I had stayed, I never would have known where my brother and mother are. You cannot share this with anyone. It may put them in danger."

Tears welled up in her eyes again as Rachel saw the anguish in Simeon's eyes. "Their secret is safe with me, Simeon. Thank you for sharing with me, my love. I know it is hard to be without family. You have my family, our friends and me. We can make a family of our own. Perhaps, somehow, we can see them again."

Simeon just slowly shook his head and looked at the floor.

Rachel told of selling Thomas' pottery and promising the regulars that Simeon would continue the work, so that they would not go elsewhere. She rested her head on his shoulder, and they just sat there in front of the small fire listening to the rain. Simeon felt her warm body next to his and quietly thanked Yahweh for such an understanding woman. Simeon realized that it was easy to talk to Yahweh, even if he wasn't a priest …something Thomas had taught him.

***

The next morning, Simeon met with Nadab and he assured Simeon that there would be a proper service for Thomas. Others were there and offered their condolences to Simeon, and he was a little surprised that they were so kind and respectful since he had heard so many dreadful reports regarding the temple scribes and priests. He didn't notice the aloof attitude of those who did not join in the meeting. They stood in the background whispering their disapproval of such a fuss over an old rabbi gone badly.

Later that same day, Simeon met with Seth and Irad, and they planned the rest of the day at the shop. There were no pieces left to dry or fire, so Seth and Irad kept busy by bringing Simeon clay to work. Simeon worked tirelessly to make-up for the lack of turned pieces. He made a variety of pieces to be sure he could satisfy the regulars, but he never sacrificed the quality of his work for he knew that being a master potter required consistency and no defective pieces for competitors to show. Simeon began his work with a fervor that Seth and Irad had never witnessed before.

Rachel worked in front of the shop selling and taking orders for a pot or vase that the customers wanted but was unavailable. The regulars were very understanding and treated Rachel very well for a woman. She had earned their respect.

Simeon asked the old man with the white hair to keep the clay coming. He even paid him a premium to make a few extra deliveries. The old man was happy to earn the extra money, but made it clear he didn't want to do this all the time. Simeon assured him, that it was temporary until they caught-up.

At nights, Simeon was exhausted, but he took the time to visit Thomas' grave during evening walks with Rachel. As the wedding approached, Simeon slowed down a little. He was nervous about the wedding and needed some time to think about what he was doing. Like most men, he was more afraid than he let on. Irad and Seth teased him. Nadab even teased a little.

News of the memorial service spread by word-of-mouth, and many of Thomas' old students attended. The Sadducees figured there was no risk since Thomas was now dead and would never confront them again. Nadab was eloquent in his praise for the fallen rabbi and obviously sincere. Although Nadab was ambitious and a good politician like the other priests and teachers of the law, his heart had a kindness that Simeon respected. Leaders and followers alike respected the young priest and teacher of the law. Nadab and Simeon were good friends who shared many religious discussions and debated the merits of political viewpoints. Both reviled the Romans.

Months later, the evening arrived for Rachel and Simeon to wed. It was cool outside, and the sky was clear. Rachel busily worked to prepare herself to greet Simeon under the canopy. Inside, she could hear the men talking and the crowd gathering, but her mind was elsewhere. It kept drifting to Thomas. She missed him and wondered what Thomas wanted to say so badly when he lost his speech. She knew the message was for Simeon, but Thomas looked her in the eyes as if to say, *"Take care of my beloved son."*

Her mind raced. *Oh, how I wish Thomas could see this. He loved Naomi so much. I hope Simeon loves me like that. I wish Thomas were here.*

Simeon, Irad, Nadab and Seth changed clothes in a tiny room. There was hardly enough room to turn around. They laughed and joked about the room and about it being too late to back out. Simeon laughed just as loud as the others, but deep down inside he was incredibly nervous. He wanted Rachel to like the room he had built onto the shop for the two of them, and he wanted Rachel to like the wedding ceremony and weeklong celebration. He wanted Rachel to... well... he wanted Rachel! The intensity of his love for her grew each time he spoke to her. He really couldn't care less how the wedding went. He just wanted it to be over and begin spending his life with Rachel.

Rachel was beautiful in the wedding dress that Aiko had made for her. She wore flowers in her dark, straight hair that were unlike any others. Aiko had brought some seeds from her homeland for this specific purpose. Rachel smiled at Simeon with her almond eyes and won his heart again with every smile. She seemed to glow with a happiness that surpassed anything he had seen. Too many times sadness had entered Simeon's life, and now he found a happiness that filled him with an inner peace. At last he was not alone. He would spend the rest of his days with the one he loved. He was not married out of convenience or tradition, but an affection that surpassed understanding. Oh, if only everyone could have such joy.

Nadab married them, as Simeon stood nearly comatose. He hardly heard a word spoken except Rachel's promise. Officially, the celebration began with Enoch and Rachel's first kiss. Embarrassed, Simeon took his bride's hand and the dancing began.

Dancing, singing and drinking good wine, poured from pitchers made by Simeon and Thomas, were all a part of the fun. Irad, Seth and their families were there along with many of Rachel's friends from her childhood, but not a soul was there from Simeon's former life. He dared not send a message to his mother and brother for fear of revealing their whereabouts to the Romans. The old life was finished, and the new life begun.

Simeon and Rachel were all smiles when the girls lit their lamps and lined the street from the outdoor canopy to the pottery shop. Consistent with tradition, Simeon had prepared a place for his bride. The girls all knew where it was and formed a line from the canopy to the pottery shop, lighting the way with lamps. Of course, Rachel knew too, but it was not proper to let on. Rachel feigned surprise as they entered the shop. There, next to Thomas' old room, was a new room prepared for the bride by the bridegroom. Simeon looked proudly into Rachel's eyes for her approval. She smiled back her warmest smile. Both were content to have a place of their own no matter how small.

Honest affection filled their first night. Rachel and Simeon shared intimate secrets with each other, caressing and bonding as a husband and wife. The evening was wonderful, a time filled with joy and celebration. No couple could have been happier. The world was a joyful place, and it was theirs for a night.

As the days passed after the wedding, Simeon created his own 'routine' just as Thomas had. Being a master potter required a discipline that only a few could handle. The steady work was a blessing to Rachel, because she knew he would be home for supper and would continue his studies of the scripture, something she respected very much. Simeon asked his good friend, Nadab, over occasionally so they could discuss scripture and politics together. They remained good friends.

A few days later, Simeon finally began analysis of the vase he had purchased from the merchant in Alexandria. The clay was nearly white and finer grained than the clay he used from the Jordan, which surprised him. Ah, but the paint was something he had only seen on the finest materials, but after that, he had to place it back on the shelf while he worked at the wheel to catch up.

Rachel and Simeon longed for a child, of course, and Rachel was eager to please her husband. Six months passed before Rachel came to her husband with news of a child on the way. "What wonderful news," Simeon whispered in her ear as he lifted her from the ground and twirled her around in his arms. "We need to tell the others!"

"Wait!" Rachel said as she tugged at Simeon's sleeve as he headed for the front of the shop. "We need to tell my parents first, or they will be offended, or at least my mother will be offended."

"You're right. Let's go!" They both went next-door hand-in-hand with smiles of delight on their faces. When they entered the house of Jared, Aiko greeted them and smiled. A mother's intuition is an asset for she knew immediately what was up but feigned ignorance.

"You say you have good news? Well, what might this good news be?" she asked.

Rachel answered, "Oh, mother, we're going to have a baby!" The delight was undeniable. Rachel seemed to glow, as only a pregnant woman can, and Aiko beamed like any grandmother-to-be.

Aiko and Rachel hugged and kissed each other in delight while Simeon stood there gazing at the two of them and thought, *"It doesn't get any better than this."*

That night, Rachel and Simeon both dreamed of little children running around the pottery shop.

A young carpenter learned the trade from his father as he grew into a strong young man, well versed in scripture. The citizens of Nazareth had no idea their town would be remembered for centuries as the home of this humble carpenter.

Chapter 17

Marcus had finished his assignment in Galilee. He was satisfied that he had eradicated the terrorists from the region, and it was time to move on. Those left in the area could deal with any repercussions from the elimination of the terrorists and their families. He gathered his men and prepared to move out.

"Anthony, have the men pack their belongings and prepare for the trip to Jerusalem. We have new assignments there."

"Yes sir. May I ask why Jerusalem?"

"Actually, I don't know, Anthony. All I know is that I need to report to Jerusalem after my work here is done. I regret losing two men. Although beautiful, this is a nasty place, Anthony. I would return to Rome if I could."

" I will get the men started, sir."

"See to it that they don't fool around."

"Yes sir."

Anthony exited the tent and approached the fire where the men gathered while awaiting orders. "Pack up men. We leave for Jerusalem in four hours. don't waste any time. We need to be on our way." The men responded well and began to assemble their gear and take down the tents. In less than three hours, they were ready to go.

Before they departed, Centurion Octavian, in charge of those stationed permanently in Galilee, approached Marcus, as he stood beside his horse ready to mount. "I have deep concerns about more uprisings after you're gone, and I have my troops spread over the north shore of the lake."

"There are always detachments like mine that can come and help you," Marcus assured him. "I believed that those who caused unrest are now resting themselves and that the few who escaped will not return. The remaining fishermen are probably honest men glad to see the Zealots gone. What I see here is peaceful for the most part. If you have trouble, send me a message, and I will be sure to forward it on to headquarters quickly and with the highest priority. I can understand your concern."

"Thank you, Marcus. I wish you safety on your trip and success in Jerusalem. I will send a favorable report from here."

"Goodbye, Octavian, I must go, my men are waiting."

Marcus signaled his men to begin the march to Jerusalem, and the small detachment of crack troops withdrew from Galilee. Marcus rode his horse next to Anthony, and they remained quiet as they rounded the lake. Marcus wondered what awaited them in Jerusalem.

Chapter 18

Nathan and Enoch found work quickly. A Jewish fisherman in Alexandria discovered them immediately and was happy to hire fellow Jews to work with his Jewish crew. They could scoff at the statue of Poseidon atop the Pharos each time they left the port without fear of retribution. Enoch and Nathan scoffed at nothing. They figured they were in enough trouble already.

After a few days of fishing with the crew, Nathan approached Enoch with a concerned look on his face. "Enoch, your mother and I would like to marry. She needs a real husband to protect her and she needs acceptance by the other women. Would that be okay with you?" Nathan could not adequately express his love for Esther, but it ran very deep. He had never really cared for women much, but Esther had proved his match, and he loved her for it.

If there were ever a time Enoch almost smiled, this was it. "Of course you can, Nathan. I can understand my mother's need for companionship. The women here in this tight-net Jewish neighborhood will never accept her if she is not married properly. Have you found a rabbi who will marry you?"

Nathan responded with his head down, "No, I was hoping the other fishermen could help us locate someone we could trust."

"Good idea! Wait a couple of weeks and see who we can trust, and then ask. Do you think it is okay to wait that long?"

"We certainly can. We must not wait too long or people will talk."

The two worked a week and realized that everyone on the boat seemed trustworthy. Nathan finally asked one of the fishermen about a rabbi, and he indicated that the Rabbi Benjamin from Tarsus would be a good candidate for their wedding. They described the rabbi as a man in his mid-thirties who knew scripture well and understood the hardships of being a Jew in Alexandria.

The next week, Esther and Nathan were wed in a small ceremony with a few fishermen present. Enoch was pleased to see his mother at ease and smiling again. It seemed that the whole fishing boat was his family now and yet, something was seriously missing from his life. Enoch had an unsettled feeling in Alexandria that he figured would never go away. He was a stranger in a very strange land.

Esther and Nathan rented a small place near the port among the rest of the fishermen and dockworkers, while Enoch rented a small room above a tackle shop owned by a relative of one of the fishermen. Enoch's life settled into a simple acceptance of fate.

Enoch and Nathan saw Roman's regularly. Some were seamen and others were foot soldiers like those back home. Enoch never looked them in the eyes and usually ducked into a shop or alleyway whenever he could, while Nathan just went about his business as usual and was content in Alexandria. He had no crew of his own, but enjoyed the others he worked with. The tension of working with Lamech was gone as well as the Zealots. The nets were strong and seldom needed mending. The ship was large and very seaworthy.

Chapter 19

Rachel was especially happy and cheerful while she carried the baby. Simeon worked diligently but made time to talk to her in the evenings. Life was good.

The business went well, and although Thomas was gone, the regulars came back to buy Simeon's work and encouraged him since they knew the situation. More customers came as the town grew, and the regulars recommended Simeon's shop. Seth and Irad stayed the same no matter what. They seemed content with their work and wages. Jokes and riddles abounded, and finally Simeon could relax a little as they slowly caught up and actually created some finished inventory.

Months passed as Simeon continued to establish himself as a master potter. The hours were hard, but Simeon and Rachel continued to talk to each other and keep the flame of their love alive despite the pressures of running the business. The household seemed to anticipate the arrival of their first child, and that prompted Rachel to notice the children of other young couples who visited the shop. Every time she saw a little one, she asked about its care, and the mother was always delighted to offer advice.

Late one afternoon, Rachel entered the shop and saw the vase from Alexandria sitting on the top shelf way back in the corner perched on top of the wad of cloth that came with it. Rachel approached Simeon as he ate his lunch and said, "You haven't mentioned the vase for months," tilting her head toward the distant shelf. "Remember when you mentioned it every day? You have some time now. Why don't you take a look at it and try to figure it out?"

Simeon glanced up at the dusty vase and studied it thoughtfully as he chewed his goat meat. "Good idea Rachel. Perhaps it is time I got back to what was once a passion. Maybe I can get some help from the goldsmith at the top of the hill. I used to think the big city was a waste, but now I know how much more is available here. I will see him tomorrow. I am sure he can tell me why the paint is so brilliant and if the gold in the paint is really gold."

"Oh, I sure hope it is real," interjected Rachel. "But that is a good start. I will have breakfast early tomorrow, and you can begin before the shop opens. Do you know where to find the goldsmith's shop?"

"I think so. Is it at the top of the hill just beyond the priest's and the first street to the right?"

The next morning, Simeon started his day in the usual way, but in his prayers, he asked guidance in analyzing the eastern pottery. He wanted to learn its secret. Surely, Yahweh would understand.

The goldsmith was a pleasant man although he was not Jewish. His name was Justin, and he learned his trade in Macedonia. "Ah! What beautiful workmanship! Too bad it is broken in so many pieces."

"Yes, I had to break it to analyze the clay."

"That seems a shame. It must have cost you a fortune. Do you have others like this?"

"Yes, we have one more in the family."

The goldsmith stepped back a little and said, "I recognize you. You are Simeon the potter. My wife shops at your place and buys your pottery. She has mentioned it often but never brought anything home like this! That's some tough competition!"

"Well, it would be, but it seems quite rare," replied Simeon. "I want to analyze the piece and thought you could tell me if the gold is real?"

"That can be done, but you will waste some gold. Are you willing to part with a little gold? It can pay part of your bill."

"Yes, how much will the analysis of the gold cost?" Simeon asked, hoping not to hear the "special price" thing again.

"Well, less than one drachma will be enough if I can also keep some of the gold, should it be gold."

"It's a deal."

With that, Justin took two pieces of the pottery to the back of the shop and Simeon followed. Justin carefully scraped some of the paint from the largest broken piece. "The red paint presents a problem for me. I want only gold, no other paint," he explained as he continued to work. He placed the piece under a glass that magnified the area he scraped. Carefully he scuffed some red paint away and went for the gold coloring. It was a painstaking process and took nearly an hour.

Finally, Simeon had to excuse himself and open the shop. He knew he could return after Rachel cleaned up from breakfast. As he entered the shop, Rachel asked, "Did you find the goldsmith?"

"Yes, I found him alright. He started the analysis right away, but I finally had to leave to open the shop. Can you watch the shop for a while after lunch, so I can go back and see what he discovers?"

"Sure. Just don't stay all afternoon. You know the customers want to see you?"

"Don't worry, I won't stay long."

After lunch, Simeon returned to the goldsmith's shop to check on the piece.

Justin had indeed taken some of the gold and apologized for so much being gone. He began to explain to Simeon, "I needed a fairly large sample for analysis, and the gold lines on the vase are very thin. I have completed the measurements but have not finished the calculations. Do you want to wait while I work this out?"

"If that is acceptable to you," replied Simeon.

By the time Justin finished his calculations, two more hours had passed. Justin looked up and said, "It certainly could be gold. One more test." He extracted a sliver of gold from a tiny tray, held it between tongs and then lit a small strange smelling incense stick. Holding the sample over the flame, he tilted his head and observed the sample. Then, he snuffed out the stick.

"I have good news for you. This really *is* gold. Not much, mind you, but there is a very thin layer of gold underneath and around the red paint forming the lines of decoration."

Both Simeon and Justin smiled with self-satisfaction. Simeon was right in believing it was gold, and Justin got the bonus he had expected.

"You are certainly a fortunate young man. What are you going to do now? Take the gold from the pieces and cash it in?"

"Oh! No! I am going to make a pot like this. Even if only one, it is my dream. Perhaps I can perfect the process also. I'd like to travel to the East and learn from whoever makes these, but I could spend my life looking, and I have a wife who is expecting a child. I cannot go, but I can experiment all I want."

"I wish you good fortune, Simeon. If you need me again, I will give you a special price."

Simeon nearly burst out laughing but held back. "Thank you, kind sir. I will send any customers I may find your way."

"That won't be a problem. I am the only act in town!"

"Shalom."

"Shalom, my friend."

Simeon returned to the pottery shop. On the way, he wondered where he would get gold to make such a thing. *Perhaps I can extract some from the fragments of the broken pot, but that probably would not be enough. And, oh, if I waste some gold while fooling around and not knowing what I am doing! That would be terrible. My customers are not the wealthy kind. I will have to be very careful.'*

Simeon entered the shop. "Rachel, I'm home."

Rachel met him with a hug and asked, "What did the goldsmith say?"

Simeon recounted the trip in detail. He expressed his concern that he had no way of knowing where to find gold for his experiment, and if he found it, he could probably not afford it.

Rachel chuckled. "I know where there is lots of gold. In the temple! And I know who could probably get some if you make the vase, or whatever, for the temple."

"Nadab!" They both said it in unison and nearly danced with joy.

Chapter 20

Marcus and his troops arrived in Jerusalem with no incidents. It was an easy trip.

He gave the men a much-deserved furlough, and Marcus used his first day to arrange his belongings in the barracks and to do some mending. The second day he explored the shops of Jerusalem. He heard good things about the workmanship of the Jewish artisans and the cunning of the Jewish merchants. He wanted to experience it firsthand.

While walking through the streets he noticed that the shop owners kept the streets well swept in hopes of attracting business to their street. Although the streets were never level in this hillside city, it never bothered any of the merchants since they would just form a level shelf for their merchandise with wooden planks. Items were stacked as high as possible, and Marcus noticed the champion of stackers was a basket maker. Baskets were stacked neatly as far as one could reach and then some. The short, stocky man could flip a basket either into the stack or out of the stack with great precision using what appeared to be a willow branch. Marcus watched him a good half-hour as the man hawked his goods.

Nearly everywhere, men or women sat on the ground with an assortment of foods prepared in every imaginable way. The fish were fried, baked and, most commonly, dried. The vegetables were fresh and bundled. Marcus wondered if the ones in the middle were of lesser quality but decided not to buy some to find out. After all, the Roman army fed him.

He came to the pottery shop of Simeon, stopped for a moment to look over the variety of pots, jugs and vases, and was amazed at their diversity. Some of the items were strange to Marcus, and he decided they were for some Jewish purpose. Rachael came out to greet him and held up an exquisite pitcher.

"For your room sir?" She asked.

Marcus thought about his new apartment and realized that there were no cups, no pitcher and no bowl. "Well this may be something I need after all. Do you have a couple of cups and washbowl to go with it?"

"Of course," she replied."

It was then he noticed she was pregnant but knew better than to say anything. She went inside and disappeared. Then out came a man, Irad, with two cups, and a fine-looking bowl. "Is this what you are looking for, Sir?" Irad asked.

"Yes, that will be fine, depending on the price of course."

"You are an officer, am I correct?"

"Yes."

"For officers, we have a special price."

"So, what is this special price?"

"Let me see, I need to add it up," Irad explained as he scratched his head and looked over the merchandise. "I think we can sell it to you for only one piece of silver. That seems about right."

Marcus wanted to laugh. The Romans didn't do business with prices that seemed "about right", but he just smiled and agreed since it was less than he would have spent in Rome, and the pottery seemed better than any he had seen in Palestine. He started to gather up his purchase and realized that a basket would be a good idea. "Wait here just a moment while I get something to carry it in."

"That will be fine. There is a basket merchant just up the hill a little way."

Marcus walked up to the stocky basket man and, just for the entertainment, requested a large basket near the bottom of a stack. Without a moment's hesitation, the man took his stick and gently pried up the stack, pulled out the basket and then lowered the stack in place, never once touching any basket but the one he sold to Marcus. Again, Marcus smiled at the Jewish basket man.

Marcus returned from his shopping, set his new acquisitions down on the lone table in his room and plopped down on the mat. Shopping had worn him out.

The next day, Marcus wandered the streets of Jerusalem and admired the temple and the surrounding buildings built by Herod, his detestable old boss. The buildings were beautiful and at the same time crude. He could only compare them to the structures he had seen in Rome which were indeed magnificent. Yet, something about the architecture in Jerusalem made it unique and admirable. Just the fact that it was here amazed him. The valley was certainly better than most, and the hill was suitable for a city, but the weather was awful, and the Jordan River just didn't seem especially impressive. Marcus knew that ancestors must have picked this place and settled here, but why? Why here?

Marcus stopped by a tailor shop. "This is certainly fine cloth and good workmanship," he told the shop owner. "You must do a brisk business."

The tailor smiled. "Indeed, I do. Most of the officials of Pilate's court come here for their clothing. I serve Rome well."

"I will need your service also. You have no problem with that, I assume." Marcus gave the man a look that only a Roman officer could provide.

"I would be honored to serve you," the tailor replied.

"Good, I will see you tomorrow. You know where to find me. Ask for Marcus." Marcus turned and moved on to investigate some more shops.

Then he approached the tent of a leather worker. "I have a small detachment of men who will need some repairs. I want to know if you can do the work."

"How many?"

"Twenty. And only about half need repairs."

"Yes. I can accommodate you. The shop has enough workers to repair four or five items a day. Is that enough?"

"That will be fine."

"My prices are posted and apply to all visitors, Romans or my Jewish friends. I do not offer special prices like many. I prefer to do business that way, and it often attracts business for me."

"I like your attitude. I'll send my supply officer. His name is Eric. He is light-haired, fair-skinned and **BIG**."

Marcus laughed as he thought how intimidating Eric could be and thought, *I bet we get a special price after all.*

Marcus moved on to other shops. He knew that the Jews were disciplined, devout, and sometimes extreme in their beliefs, but he wished he had something like that to believe in. He had only believed in himself for so long that it was almost a religion. Most Roman soldiers were that way, but as they grew older, many searched for something more than themselves and usually ended-up empty handed. Marcus was growing older, and he felt it. He would like to sit down with a Jew sometime and just talk amicably, but it was unlikely to happen. Their hatred for the western kingdom ran deep. Perhaps the tailor was a viable candidate.

Marcus made his way back to the barracks where his troops were staying. The quarters were wonderfully comfortable, and Marcus considered it a privilege to have such a solid roof over his head. When he arrived, a neatly folded note was lying on his bench. Opening the note, Marcus read:

"Immediately report to the outer chamber of Pontius Pilate's quarters for further instructions."

Marcus was stunned. *What could this mean? I have not even met Pilate. I am not appropriately dressed.* He looked around. No others were in the barracks. Quickly, he slipped into full officer's dress and grabbed his helmet. He knew better than to appear before Pontius Pilate in a tattered uniform even if it was clean. It could end his career.

It was only a short walk to the outer chamber of Pilate's quarters. The attendant at the door blocked his entry until Marcus presented the note with Pilate's own seal. The attendant then entered the room followed by Marcus. The guard told Marcus to stand fast while the attendant entered Pilate's chambers and announced Marcus.

Marcus entered the lavish chamber, easily big enough for his company of twenty men. There was Pilate reclined at an ornate table with his wife and a few servants in attendance. The Tribune was seated near Pilate.

"Marcus, I have good news for you," began Pilate. "You have done an excellent job for both Herod and now Antipas, his son. You have shown yourself a capable leader and able to keep peace with the general population while weeding-out the chaff of society. I have a recommendation from the Tribune for your promotion to Centurion. If you accept, you will direct our operations here in Jerusalem under the Tribune. Do you accept?"

Marcus knew he must answer yes, but he had little idea what he meant by "operations in Jerusalem."

"Yes. I accept Your Excellency's assignment."

"Fine, you will report here at dawn tomorrow, and the Tribune will have other officers here to instruct you in the affairs of Jerusalem, and I will explain, personally, what I expect of you. Understand?"

"Yes sir."

"You are dismissed."

That was the shortest conversation Marcus ever had with a superior, especially a politician. Pilate apparently spoke plainly. The furlough was over, and Marcus knew he would receive some serious instruction to begin a task that was notoriously difficult. That night Marcus slept fitfully dreaming about mobs of Jews, a burning Jerusalem, and an angry Governor.

***

The next morning, Marcus began his review with four other officers. Jason, a Centurion himself, attended earlier training with Marcus and was a good friend. The other three younger officers seemed to have less interest in the work and were mostly interested in drinking.

"Marcus," Jason began, "I heard that you were coming, and I'm pleased you are here."

"Jason! It's good to see you, my friend. How are the wife and children?"

"Great," replied Jason, happy to see his friend after many years.

"During the briefing you mentioned a fear of further discontent here in Jerusalem. What, exactly, makes you feel that way?" asked Marcus.

"The land is always full of Jewish self-proclaimed prophets, and there is one who preaches repentance that the people adore. It is never good when this happens because there is always violence that follows. His name is John, and he lives in the wilderness eating honey, locusts, and other wild things. He avoids the towns."

"Where, exactly, does he operate? "

"He preaches along the Jordan between the north shore of the Dead Sea and Bethabara. This year about half of the farmers will let the farmland rest, and they are now available to listen to him. He insults Herod Antipas, which you know is extremely dangerous."

"Sounds like he shares the opinion of most of the farmers and city dwellers alike," chided Marcus.

"The problem is that he seems to know the activities of Herod and his family and protests their behavior. Of course, he's right to complain, but this goes further than that. He says that the wrath of God will be upon them and stirs up the people against Herod. I fear some sort of rebellion."

"Jason, we can't stomp on every idiot that complains. How big is his following?"

"It is small, perhaps a hundred people, at most. It is just that I don't like this sort of thing, and it seems so strange to me. What on earth could he possibly accomplish except to stir up the people?"

"Well, probably nothing more than just that. If Herod is angry enough, he will probably take care of it himself. In fact, he may just call on you, Jason, to take care of it. You have that area. At any rate, keep me informed. My assignment is Jerusalem. If he heads this way, let me know. I haven't received orders from Pilate yet."

There was a long pause before Marcus continued. "Send a messenger if you have need of some support. I don't believe anybody is going to give you much trouble around here after what we just did in Galilee. They ought to be particularly respectful. If you need to speak to this John, do so."

"I wouldn't dare talk to this man. It would just turn him against Rome. We have enough of that now. I'll let headquarters know if we need help, but I think we can handle it. I just wanted you to know."

"Thanks, Jason. You are a good man and a good Roman. I'm sure you'll do whatever is right."

Jason turned and left with a brief wave. They had been friends a long time, and both respected each other as good leaders and sensible men.

Marcus moved his men into formation shortly after the conversation with Jason. He said goodbye to them and returned to the barracks. Marcus knew his men would enjoy the city and its benefits. He doubted if there was much of an assignment waiting for them in Jerusalem. Things were relatively quiet for it being such a hotbed of Jewish fanaticism. Now, it seemed the fundamentalists were in the surrounding countryside, and the ruling Jews in Jerusalem kept tight rein on their people by keeping them busy with feasts and trade in the temple. The priests were politically savvy about what to say and do.

Marcus straightened his uniform and headed for Pilate's quarters.

John's ministry began as he traveled along the Jordan to call for repentance. The people responded with kindness, but the scribes and teachers of the law objected. John spoke more boldly the more boldly they objected.

Chapter 21

Rachel's eyes were wide and filled with fear. The
midwife told her to ease up and hold back. Rachel
struggled to hold back, but with little success. The
pains were coming so fast they took control of her body.
The baby was not coming, and Rachel knew something was
wrong. "Simeonnnn!" she screamed. She was drenched in
sweat and clutching the mat. Her long dark hair was all
over her face. She closed her eyes and pushed hard.

Jared restrained Simeon by grabbing his arm. "Sit
down Simeon. We men can do nothing. She is a strong
young woman and has a good midwife. They all scream
like this at the end."

Simeon had never heard anyone scream like that with
the possible exception of his mother when the Romans
killed his father. Inside, he wanted to scream too. There
was something wrong and he knew it. He plopped down

on the bench and ran his strong fingers through his sweaty hair. It seemed ridiculously hot.

Soon it became quiet. There was no sound coming from the room. No more screams and no more scurrying around. The midwife came out with an ashen look on her face. She shook her head and asked for Aiko. Aiko rose from the corner where she was huddled and hurried across the room and through the curtain with the midwife.

A half-hour later, Aiko summoned Simeon, and he slowly rose with Jared close behind. As he entered the room, there was Rachel motionless on the bed. Blood was everywhere, and both men knew it had gone badly. Simeon looked at Aiko as she spoke. "She is just asleep, Simeon. She has lost a lot of blood. Only Yahweh knows what is next. We can only wait."

Simeon knelt by Rachel on the mat. He moved close to her and whispered, "I'll wait here." Then, looking up at the midwife, he asked," What about the baby?"

"The baby is gone," the midwife abruptly answered.

Tears ran down Aiko's cheeks, and Jared gently took her out of the room. Simeon turned to Rachel and swept the hair out of her face.

The night was moonlit, and a gently breeze filled the room. Simeon was thankful for any relief from the heat. He asked the midwife for some cool water, wine, and a cloth.

The midwife obliged but stayed close to help with Rachel. Eventually the bleeding ceased and Simeon excused the midwife. She could only pray from here on.

Simeon stayed by Rachel for the next two days as fever rose each night and subsided each day. At last, she woke and looked around the room. Seeing Simeon standing in the doorway, she lifted her hand and motioned him to her side. "I am sorry, Simeon. I just couldn't do it. I let you down," she whispered. Then she reached up and put her arm around his neck, pulled him close, they wept together.

"I love you, Rachel. Please don't leave me," Simeon whispered back.

"I've made it this far. I won't leave you, Simeon."

"Rest now. Here is some wine for you. It will help you sleep and help you heal," Simeon said as he poured some wine in Rachel's favorite cup, a cup that he had made especially for her months earlier.

Rachel sipped it, swallowed hard, coughed a little and then pushed it away. "Thank you, Simeon. Are Mom or Dad around?"

"Yes, I will go for them."

"No. Stay here with me. I will talk to them later." Then Rachel drifted back to sleep.

It was days before Rachel could walk again. She seemed much older and lost the enthusiastic bounce in her steps. But, slowly, she regained her strength and could walk straight and tall again. Simeon went back to work and the shop continued. There was a loss of joy in the household of Simeon. Despite their despair, the love between Rachel and Simeon grew stronger with each passing day. He was just glad she was alive. She was happy to be back with her husband and counted each day a blessing.

Chapter 22

Upon reaching Pilate's quarters, Marcus received a warm welcome. "Sit down and relax. I want to give you instructions," began the governor. "As you know, there are many who would usurp my position. I have no intention of letting it be so. The Sanhedrin has seventy-one Jewish fools who continually complain of the lack of protection. Jason arrests and executes those who offend either the Sanhedrin or Herod. Your job is to see to it that nothing happens to *me*. Understand?"

"Yes sir."

"I want you to stay here in this building, and I will supply you with a servant of your choice. You will have your one hundred men, and I promise that I will keep you busy. You will investigate any plots against me and quell them immediately. You will do nothing without my full knowledge beforehand. We must deal with my enemies

171

in a politically expedient manner. We can't just kill some of them. Others we can. But, for some, we can trump up a charge and have them put in prison. It is a nasty business. I don't like it either, but that is how it is. Can you do this?"

Marcus wanted to shout no but knew better. This was his commander, and he was a soldier after all. "Yes, sir, I can," he replied without elaborating.

"Good. Now let us get down to business," he said as he leaned forward for his cup of wine. They spent the whole day going over the political friends and enemies of Pilate. Oddly enough, most were Roman, and few were Jews. The Jews were just pawns of the state. It was obvious.

As Pilate spoke and Marcus made notes, Pilate's beautiful wife entered and stared at Marcus. "Pontius, who is your friend," she asked.

"This is Marcus, the new Centurion in charge of my security. Marcus, meet my wife," replied Pilate with a warm smile. "She is always interested in what I am doing."

Her beauty was striking but Marcus tried not to let it show. With such a beautiful wife, he was sure some of Pilates "enemies" were would-be-suitors. Pilate was no fool and neither was Marcus.

At the end of the day, a servant led Marcus to a quiet, well-appointed room with small adjoining servant's quarters. The servant instructed Marcus to select the servant of his choice and, once approved by Pilate; the servant would occupy this smaller area and be on call twenty-four hours a day. Marcus' men would be quartered nearby.

Marcus sat down and pondered the situation. *If I ask Anthony to be my servant, it would be an insult to Anthony. I will not do that! So, where can I find a suitable servant in Jerusalem? Exactly what do I want for a servant? What would a servant do? I'm not used to someone catering to me. Perhaps a Jewish servant could add to my knowledge of the Jews and prove useful in my work. Yes, a Jew!*

Chapter 23

The ship had just pulled into port. Nathan secured the ship to the dock while Enoch prepared to unload the catch. Nathan looked over the side and there stood a Roman Soldier with his hands on his hips and defiantly eyeing Nathan. "Are you in charge here?" asked the soldier.

"No," Nathan replied. "The man on the deck is our captain." Nathan pointed to the captain who looked down at the soldier in disgust. Nathan turned away as quickly as possible to avoid eye contact with the soldier lest he reveal his fear.

"We're coming aboard," shouted the soldier. "We need rations," he continued, as if that were reason enough. The soldier and two of his cohorts moved past Enoch, pushing him aside. Then turning back to Enoch, he ordered, "Load those baskets on the dock until they are full."

Enoch turned to the captain.

"Do as the man says," shouted the captain. Then, with his hands on his hips and his head raised high, the captain shouted to the soldier; "You scum think the whole world answers to your beckon call, don't you? Why not just take the boat and catch your own fish? Oh… yes… because you are too stupid to know how to catch a fish, let alone sail!" Then he spit onto the dock, barely missing the baskets.

The soldier had heard all this before. No matter. He gave Enoch a push on the chest and said, "Get to it man! We don't have all day." He stood again with his hands on his hip and feet apart, daring Enoch to give him a hard time too.

Enoch was no fool. He began unloading the smelly cargo into the baskets with the help of his fellow fishermen. Nathan pitched in too and whispered into Enoch's ear, "Don't do anything you will regret, my boy."

"Don't worry. I won't," Enoch whispered back.

The soldiers loaded their rations onto a horse drawn cart without incident and disappeared from sight. Nathan and Enoch just stood watching them go. "Tomorrow is the Sabbath," said Enoch. "I'm going to hear scripture. I feel as if I am drifting away from what my father taught me. Are you and Mother coming too, Nathan, or do I go by myself?"

"You *do* have Jewish blood, don't you? No, I have enough and want no part of it anymore. You're on your own."

"I am just sick of the Romans. They are everywhere I go and I can't get away from them. Perhaps salvation is coming. It is the only hope I have and …. I hate fishing here. I want to go back to Galilee. I liked it there and will return when I think it is safe."

"It's never safe to be a Jew. Go back, and they will hunt you down and kill you."

"We'll see!" replied Enoch as he gathered some empty baskets the Romans had left behind.

Enoch knew exactly where the synagogue was located from being in the wedding. He walked purposefully toward the small building determined to get some answers. The portly Rabbi Benjamin met him at the door, barefoot and with a bowl in his hand, "Can I help you, Enoch?" he asked.

Enoch replied that he wanted to study scripture, and that he had a specific purpose in mind. "My purpose requires me to learn as much as possible about the coming Messiah," he explained.

"Come in and we will talk. Want something to eat?"

"Yes, if you don't mind. It has been a long tedious day for me." Enoch talked for about an hour with Rabbi Benjamin about the need to know all he could find out about the Messiah because he expected him soon and wanted to join his army, provided he was convinced it was really the Messiah. Rabbi Benjamin seemed interested and offered to share some scripture with Enoch. Both men enjoyed the meal together.

From that day forward, Enoch studied the scriptures at every opportunity. He talked to Rabbi Benjamin and the rabbi even allowed Enoch to read scriptures in the rabbi's home. Enoch soon learned that Isaiah, Micah, Zechariah and even some of the Psalms had much to say about the Messiah, but Enoch didn't understand everything he read. He longed for the Messiah like other men lust for gold.

Enoch was amazed that the great prophet, Isaiah, wrote that God was tired of the festivals and finds no pleasure in the blood of bulls, lambs, and goats. The festivals and sacrifices seemed like *everything* to the priests. Enoch could understand that idols brought impurity to the city of Jerusalem. He knew Romans had polluted the whole land with their pagan worship. However, what fascinated him most was the mention of a time when there would be no more gloom for those in distress when the son is born and who will be called Wonderful, Counselor, Mighty God, Everlasting Father, and Prince of Peace from the reign of David. *Is this a sign that the Messiah would come from the line of David? I must ask Rabbi Benjamin!*

He read on, only to find Isaiah mentioning a stump of Jesse who would have the spirit of wisdom and not rule by what he sees or hears, but by righteousness. *This must be the Messiah too.* Enoch rose and went in search of Rabbi Benjamin with a heightened sense of excitement. He needed answers, and he needed them now!

Rabbi Benjamin was eating and enjoying a roast chicken when Enoch asked to speak with him.

"Come on in, Enoch. I was just finishing. What do you want?"

"I have been reading about the Messiah and wondered if the stump of Jesse was also reference to the Messiah."

"Oh, I am sure it is. You see, the Messiah will come from the lineage of David and Jesse was David's father. Essentially the scriptures are saying that he will come from the lineage of David and from the lineage of Jesse. They are the same thing. Does that answer your question?"

"Yes, but with all these descriptions it is still hard for me to imagine recognizing him from what I read. And when will he come?"

"Well, I don't know when he will come but there are certain things we know for sure. He will be born of the lineage of David and will be born in Bethlehem. Imagine, the King of the Jews being born in such a little town!"

Enoch stood up suddenly and dropped the drumstick from his hand. "What did you just say?"

"Imagine, the King of the Jews being born in such a small town"

"Rabbi…He is here! Now! Somewhere he is walking around in Judea. I know it!"

"How could you possibly be sure of such a thing, Enoch?"

"I was there when the King of the Jews was born! You know, in Bethlehem! Believe me I know, Rabbi…I know."

Rabbi Benjamin had no idea what Enoch was talking about and just looked up at him as if he were crazy.

Enoch turned to the right, hesitated, and then turned left. He didn't know what to do but had this unsettling urge to run. "I must go now. Thank you for teaching me and letting me study the scriptures with you. I am going to find the Messiah. Goodbye."

Enoch walked out of the humble dwelling and took a deep breath of fresh air.

Chapter 24

Nadab, dressed in all his priestly finery, stopped by the pottery shop to talk to Simeon. "I have been asked to be on the Sanhedrin!" he exclaimed. He was obviously excited and wanted to share his joy with someone.

"Great, Nadab! I guess we will be seeing you in the temple regularly. What an honor!" chimed Simeon. Rachel came out to see what all the commotion was about, and again Nadab sang out, "Rachel, I am going to be in the Sanhedrin!"

"Wonderful," she replied, a smile beaming on her face. "What next! I suppose you will be Chief Priest some day!"

" Well, that may be a little farfetched, but I am pleased none the less."

"Come have supper with us tonight," invited Simeon, looking at Rachel for her approval.

"Sure, come on in. You men can talk while I fix supper," she replied with a half-smile. *Here we go again. Men talk while the woman works.*

After supper, Nadab and Enoch talked of politics and discussed the latest despicable antics of Herod's family. Then, just as Rachel sat down with the men, the topic turned to a child that had visited the temple a few years back. The little boy impressed Nadab with his knowledge of scripture and Nadab could not get him out of his mind. Rachel and Simeon listened intently as he described the boy who had wandered onto the steps of the temple and began talking, unabashedly, to the scribes and priests. "He talked of great commandments and saving the people caught in a spiritual battle for their souls. Twelve-year-old boys just don't speak of such things," said Nadab.

"How do you think he became so knowledgeable?" asked Rachel.

"I don't know. At first, I thought he must be a rabbi's son or something, but then his father and mother appeared. They were commoners. He was a construction worker of all things! They can't even read."

Simeon choked on those words, knowing that he and his father could read just fine. His father was wise enough to teach him some good, yet simple, concepts that had served him well.

Rachel just sat listening patiently and said nothing.

Simeon wondered what she thought but held his tongue. Of course, he could ask later. However, Nadab beat him to the punch.

"Rachel, what do you think of a twelve-year-old rabbi?"

Rachel's eyes opened wide and she hesitated awhile. "Well, I guess he has an insight that most twelve-year-old's lack. I should be so blessed to have a son who understands such things."

The answer seemed to satisfy both men. As it grew later, Rachel retired without comment. Nadab and Simeon ran out of things to talk about, and Nadab finally returned to his quarters at the temple.

That night Nadab dreamed of leading the temple worship at the feasts and festivals.

Simeon worked at the wheel.

The next morning, Simeon started his daily routine as usual. Irad and Seth worked quietly, and Simeon began his work in earnest. Days were long now, but he made more and more pots each day. Regulars and newcomers alike revered his pitches and began to buy all their earthenware at Simeon's shop. Because of the long hours and working the clay endlessly, Simeon had sore fingers by the time the Sabbath arrived. They would heal over the Sabbath, and he would begin his work again.

This week, however, a new sore appeared on his head, of all places, just above his right ear. He couldn't understand and it worried him because of its location and appearance. He wore a long head wrap most of the time to keep the sweat out of his eyes. Therefore, he just covered it with the wrap. Simeon was sure Rachel would eventually notice but he kept it hidden as much as he could. It began to spread and so did Simeon's fear. Nothing would make it go away. He only knew of a few things to try, but nothing seemed to work. Finally, Rachel noticed.

"Simeon, do you know you have a sore on your head? It looks bad. Did you scrape it or something? The flesh seems to be broken and loose," she asked with obvious concern in her eyes.

"Oh that. Who knows where that came from? I noticed it about a day ago," Simeon lied, hoping that she would cease pursuing the topic, but no such luck.

She leaned forward and started to kiss his sore! Simeon pulled away quickly and looked her in the eye and said, "It may be infected, Rachel. Don't do that!"

"It has a smell, Simeon. I think someone should look at it."

"I will have someone look at it in a few days if it hasn't gotten better. I need to go down to the Jordan tomorrow and check on some new clay. I will have someone look at it after that." With that remark, Rachel dropped the subject and moved on. She was concerned but trusted Simeon to do as he promised.

The next day was sunny with a cool breeze and ideal for travel, so Simeon went down to the Jordan just as he had said. He slipped away to a quiet pool in the small stream and walked into the water up to his chest. He looked to the sky and began to count. "One," he whispered and submerged himself in the pool. "Two," he submerged himself again. "Three," he whispered and touched his sore. "Four." His heart began to beat faster with excitement and fear. "Five Six, Seven!" he nearly shouted. He shook his head and began to walk to the shore.

As he looked up and there on a rock sat a man in skins, with a long beard and unruly hair, eating what looked like a bug. "It won't work, you know," the man said rather matter-of-factly.

Simeon was startled to see the man and replied with an innocent look on his face, "What do you mean?"

"I mean you can't cure leprosy that way."

"I was just rinsing myself off from the heat," Simeon replied with a look of disdain. "Who are you anyway?"

"I am a voice crying in the wilderness. I call men to repentance. And who are you, but a potter with a problem?"

"How do you know I am a potter? You have never been to my shop. I would know you," Simeon replied as he walked up to shore unable to avoid the man in skins.

"Actually, it was just a guess from the look of your hands and one strong leg that moves the wheel. Yours is a peculiar trade, you know."

"And one crying in the wilderness is not?"

"Well, I suppose it is, but I am called by God to do so, and so I do. One comes after me who is far greater than I am and will call you to salvation. I need his salvation as greatly as you, my friend."

"Don't call *me* friend. You are an *idiot* crying in the wilderness. What does this have to do with me? I am just a potter who is hot. Out of my way!" The challenge angered Simeon and after being in Jerusalem for all these years, he had heard many come to preach. They were everything from Zealots to raving idiots usually calling for the overthrow of Rome. He wanted no part of this wild man who simply recognized what Simeon was doing, challenged him and wanted Simeon to hear his message. Simeon wanted no part of the man or his sermon.

"You can brush me aside and walk away, but you can't brush the leprosy from your hair, Brother. Come back, repent and be baptized in the Jordan. Look for the one who is coming who can wash away your sins with the words of his mouth. Whatever you do, don't brush *him* aside!" With that, the man turned and walked downstream, with his face lifted up as if basking in the sun.

Simeon lifted his hand once more to his head. The detestable sore was still there. Nothing…the man was right. The dipping failed to make any difference.

Simeon's clothes dried quickly in the sun and breeze as he walked back to Jerusalem. He pondered what to do about the sore and decided he could not go to the priest up the hill for fear of him declaring Simeon a leper. Yet, he wondered whom he could trust. Jared was the only one he could think of, but Jared was Rachel's father and Jared would be inclined to take the careful route.

Perhaps that wasn't so bad after all. Rachel was the most important person in Jared's life as well as Simeon's. Neither man would want to put her at risk. *How could this be happening to me? All my life I have been good, and I listened to Thomas. I am faithful and true to Rachel. I am kind to my customers. What has brought this on? It does not seem fair to me. What will Jared say? Will he run me out, or what? I really don't want to go back.'*

Nevertheless, Simeon plodded home to Jerusalem, head bent down in futile self-debate and went directly to Jared's house avoiding his shop. It was after sunset, and

Jared was home. He asked Aiko for Jared and then asked Jared to go for a walk with him. Jared could see the deep concern on Simeon's face and followed him out of the door. They walked down the hill toward the outskirts of town and out of the light before Simeon spoke, "I have something I need to ask you Jared. I have a problem, and I need your advice."

Jared stiffened, wondering what was wrong with what seemed to him to be the perfect life. "I'm here to listen, Simeon," he replied.

"I have noticed a sore on the side of my head, and I don't know what to do about it. It will not go away, and I am ignorant of what it could be. I am afraid to see the doctor or the priest for fear that it may be something that will cause the priest to send me away. Yet, I want to protect Rachel from any risk. You know I love her dearly. She went through a terrible time losing the baby. I will not put her through any more. What do you think I should do, Jared?"

"Let me take a look at it, Simeon. Perhaps I have seen something like it before and it is nothing. Yet, I had an uncle who had leprosy, and I know what he went through. I'll recognize it. Pray you are not Leprous. If you are, your life is over my son. Come on home with me, and I will look at it in the light of the lamp. We will not let Aiko know what we're doing."

Simeon's head dropped even farther and sweat dripped from his brow. He could feel his heartbeat as it had done before when he thought about leprosy. Anything but that!

They turned around on the path and both silently walked home. It was not a long walk, but it seemed like an eternity. Simeon wondered if he had done the right thing, but if Jared could tell what it was, or was not, it would help. Now, more than ever, Simeon knew what it was to pray for mercy. Thomas had often mentioned praying for mercy and mentioned it in reference to his wife. He had never mentioned how she died and Simeon had never asked. Just the mention of death made him shudder.

They arrived back at Jared's house and Aiko had already gone to bed and sounded as if she was sound asleep behind their curtain. Jared asked Simeon to sit on the floor, and Jared stood behind him with a lamp in his hand. Jared knew it was a risk to touch the sore so he parted Simeon's hair with a wooden stick that Aiko used to light the lamps. As the hair parted, he could see bits and pieces of flesh fall to Simeon's shoulder.

The sore was red in the center with an ashen color around it. The hair was gone from the area where the sore was, and it was obvious that some had fallen out. Jared knew that the final test would be the smell. His uncle had a horrible smell about him when Jared would take food to him as a boy. He would sneak it to his uncle until his father found out and severely punished him. He looked closely and then moved his nose closer to Simeon's head hoping that Simeon would not know what he was doing.

There it was… the horrible smell. Jared's heart sank. He didn't want to be the one to tell Simeon and yet his daughter's life was at risk. *Oh please. Let me be wrong about this.* Jared stopped looking and walked slowly around Simeon. Simeon looked up. His face was dripping with sweat, and he was taking short, shallow breaths.

"Where did you go today, Simeon?"

"I went to the Jordan. To a small pool where I thought no one would see me and dipped myself in the Jordan seven times like Naaman. I hoped it would help, but it didn't."

"Simeon, I had an uncle who had leprosy and I know it only from the smell. I am not sure, but the smell of your sore is very similar. I think you need to see the priest."

Herod Antipas grew more and more powerful as he eliminated his enemies and grew notorious for his cruelty. As he sat in the palace and watched Salome's every move, his lust for her grew until it surpassed by his lust for power.

Chapter 25

Marcus instructed Anthony to find him a suitable servant that could help with the household chores, paperwork and intelligence. He only suggested a Jew, but Anthony knew his commander enough to know what a suggestion meant.

After asking around for a day, Anthony found a man in his late forties with a humble spirit and didn't seem filled with hate for the Romans. He was a patient man and a Levite, so he would know the meanings of the festivals and what was going on in the minds of the Jews; a good choice.

Marcus talked to the man. "Tell me Aaron, why are you willing to serve a Roman?"

Marcus minced no words.

"I serve for two reasons. First, a bitter Sadducee priest rejected me and sold me into slavery. A rabbi named Thomas taught me about the Messiah and life after death, but the Sadducees, those in charge, didn't agree with what Thomas taught. I objected, and now, we are both abandoned. Secondly, I do not hate anyone, Roman or not. Many times in history, other nations conquered we Jews, usually because we drifted away from our God and deserved it. This lesson is a hard lesson for us Jews. But you and your men are seen by me as instruments used to call us to repentance."

"Are you saying that I and my men are but some insignificant irritation, used by your god to cleanse your people of some wrongdoing?" asked Marcus.

"Do you find that offensive?"

"Yes, but it is an honest answer. We can try this out for a time. You can tell me more about your laws and prophets, so I understand more. You have many prophets. I see them all the time."

"All are not prophets who claim to be."

Marcus turned to Anthony, "You have done a good job. I assume he can read and write."

"Quite well," Anthony responded.

"Then get him situated. I have things to do."

Actually, Marcus had nothing to do. The assignment was boring compared to the work he was used to doing. He missed the horses, travel and combat, but the intrigue was also of interest to him. It was a new kind of combat, although one he would soon learn was difficult and not very satisfying. One never knows if the battle has been won or lost.

Anthony instructed Aaron. "To reveal *any* of Marcus' plans is punishable by death, no matter how insignificant it may be," began Anthony. " we're not here to conquer, that is already accomplished. We are here to keep the peace. I know Marcus wants to understand the traditions of the Jews. That is one of the reasons I selected you. Cooperate with Marcus, or your stay here will certainly be short."

Aaron seemed willing to serve and he quickly agreed. For a slave, the quarters were great!

As Anthony walked back to Marcus' room, a guard stopped him and said, "The Governor wants to see Marcus...now!"

Anthony hurried his steps and knocked politely on Marcus' door. He entered and respectfully relayed the message.

"I wonder what this is about. Come with me Anthony, I want you to meet the Governor, if he will have you," responded Marcus.

Anthony didn't want to meet the Governor. He was not interested in such things and certainly had no use for politicians, but he followed Marcus as instructed. They approached the Governor's door, and the Governor's guard announced Marcus.

"Your Honor. You asked for me?"

"Yes, Marcus, and I didn't ask for anyone else. Get rid of him," Pilate responded angrily motioning to Anthony. Anthony turned smartly and exited the room without instruction from Marcus, which would only add to the insult.

"Marcus, I have an assignment for you. There is a certain Jew named John who is causing Herod a lot of grief, and he wants him put in prison. I exchanged a favor for him. I want you and your men to arrest this John and put him in the prison at the Fortress of Machaerus. He is called "John the Baptizer" by the Jews and dips people in the Jordan River somewhere between Bethabara and the Dead Sea. I want you on it right away."

"And his offence"

"It is none of your business, Marcus. Just do it. No, wait! Actually, you do need to know. It will help you understand this bunch of idiots. John offended Herod by calling him a murderer and his wife a whore. One just doesn't get by with such insults in these parts."

"Thank you, sir. I will begin at once," Marcus replied. He turned and exited quickly only to find Anthony just outside the door.

"Well, we certainly learned something there, didn't we?" Marcus commented.

"Yes, and I just want you to know. Do not *ever* introduce me to this man."

"I am sorry, Anthony, it was my mistake, not yours. He was in a bad mood when we arrived. Don't worry about it."

"Humph," was Anthony's only reply.

Since Marcus had talked to Jason about John who preaches in the wilderness, he summoned Jason. Jason confirmed the verbal attacks on King Herod and agreed to help Marcus and his men locate John. That very evening they headed west to the Jordan and camped the night near the river.

The next morning they observed men walking north along the riverbank and figured they headed for wherever John was preaching. Their theory was soon proven correct when they spotted a large gathering by the river. John was standing waist deep in the river addressing the people. Jason was ready to move in immediately, but Marcus stopped him. "I want to hear him to find out if he mentions Herod. It would be good to have solid evidence against him. Besides, if he calls himself a prophet, what is it he is prophesying?"

John continued preaching in a loud voice to the people. "Repent for the day of the Lord is at hand! One has come who is greater than I am. I am not fit to remove his sandals for he can cleanse you of your sins. Repent! Do not sin, for judgment is at hand. Come and be baptized in the water of the Jordan, the water of our ancestors who came to this land to claim it as our inheritance. Cleanse your body in the water as a sign of your repentance."

People slowly walked into the water and lined up beside John. He took them one by one and, raising one hand to the heavens and looking up, he dipped them into the murky Jordan with the other hand. He was strong indeed and needed only one hand for even the heaviest of men. Women also came, an unusual sight for Marcus since Aaron had told him that the Jewish women usually didn't participate in religious activity. Marcus and Jason quietly stood by with their men and witnessed the activity. John spoke nothing of Herod, but the Romans had not heard the whole sermon. It really didn't matter. Marcus had his orders.

After the sermon, John came to the west bank of the Jordan and visited with the people. His garment was made of skins and his face was like leather from the sun and wind. His smile was captivating although his teeth were badly chipped. He looked up at the Romans waiting just a little way up the hill and addressed them in the same loud voice. "Here are our conquerors. Have they come to join us or to persecute us even more?" Marcus and his men didn't reply with even so much as a nod of their head. "I see the evil in their eyes and deceit in their hearts." He walked up the shore to where they were standing. The people just stood still on the shore watching with interest and trepidation.

John spoke quietly to Marcus and Jason recognizing their rank. "Have you come to listen or to take me away?"

"We have come to take you away." Jason answered without emotion.

Again, John spoke quietly. "Then do so, but don't harm the people. They are kind, gentle people and no threat to you. Let me say some final words to them, and I will go quietly with you."

"Go ahead and speak but make it snappy and watch what you say," Marcus replied this time.

"I am going now with these men. Keep watch for the one who will come after me. You must listen to him and do as he says. Spread the word." With that John, who seemed so animated before, quietly joined the Romans as they moved south along the river. He never asked where he was going and never offered resistance. Marcus was surprised, even disappointed. A few of the men from the river followed about a kilometer down the path, but when five soldiers from Marcus' legion dropped back and confronted them, they ceased following. Nobody messes with the Roman soldiers.

A little further, down river, Jason ordered his men to bind John's wrists, and his men obeyed hastily.

Jason asked, "Where did you say we're taking him?"

Marcus replied, "There is a prison on the east bank called the Fortress of Machaerus. He will be imprisoned there, away from the crowds in Jerusalem or along the river. No one will find him there. That is why I didn't allow others to follow."

"Good move. My men will make sure no one at the prison speaks of him."

***

The Fortress of Machaerus was a desolate place. Not large, but hot and guarded by desperate soldiers with little to do except harass the prisoners, which was almost a sport.

The guards tossed John into a cell with four other men, all of which had been there a month or more. The others said nothing. They just sat against the wall downcast, unkempt and gaunt. John joined them without saying a word until the guards were gone. Then he whispered, "Have you heard the good news….."

Chapter 26

Simeon was beside himself. He sat in silence in the shop wondering what to say in the morning. He decided he would give Rachel and the others instructions before leaving for the priest's quarters at the top of the hill.

As dawn broke, Rachel appeared first, as usual. "Simeon, you never came to bed last night. What is wrong?" Simeon stood silently. "Simeon, talk to me. I need to know. You are so changed, that I don't know what to do. You always talked to me, but now you are silent. I can't stand this!" Still Simeon stood silently with his back against the wall of the shop.

"I am waiting for the others, they will be here soon. don't speak to me Rachel."

With that, Rachel started to carry the pottery outside to the front of the shop. Usually Irad did this because he was usually the first to arrive. However, this was certainly going to be an unusual day, and Rachel knew it.

Irad appeared with Seth close behind. They stood in front of Simeon as he stood there with sweat dripping from his brow and stiff as a cedar. He wore the cloth head cover down on his forehead and awkwardly down to his ears.

"Now that you are all here, I must speak to all of you at once. I must go, never to return." They all looked concerned and Rachel looked devastated. "I want you to sell all we have. Find another potter as soon as you can."

Rachel began to interrupt, but Simeon raised his hand to stop her. "Don't stop me Rachel," Simeon pleaded. "Rachel, I want you to sell the pieces of the special pottery I bought in Alexandria for the gold. You will need it. Return to your father and mother. Irad and Seth, I want you to find other work if you cannot find a potter. It may be hard to sell the shop but you must try, especially if you cannot find work soon. Split the proceeds with Jared and move on."

"Why are you doing this, Simeon? I think we all deserve an explanation," insisted Seth with some anger in his voice.

"I must go see the priest at the top of the hill, and I fear what he is going to tell me." Simeon's eyes dropped to the floor.

Rachel put her hand over her mouth and took a deep, halting breath. Her eyes were like saucers, and she took a step back. Seth, on the other hand, stepped forward. "What are you talking about, Simeon. This can't be so. I have worked with you every day, and I see no sores and neither do your customers. You need to stay! Stay and we can continue as long as we can until whatever ails you is over. Don't go there or you will surely never return."

"I can't expose Rachel any more, or you and Irad for that matter. I have seen Jared, and he believes it is leprosy, and he says I should go. Jared knows that he is right. It will not go away, and it is the mark of death for me." He gazed at the floor as he spoke.

Rachel rushed to him and Simeon held her shoulders at arm's length. "You cannot touch me, Rachel. That is why I stayed in here last night. Burn the bed and all my clothing in the kiln, and go to your father. He will understand. Sell all you can before I come down the hill, because after that you may not be able to. Take the gold to the goldsmith. He knows it is genuine. I must go now. After this, you will never see me again. I will not walk down this hill as Thomas' friend did all those years ago. Never!"

Simeon turned and exited the back door of the shop. As he passed the ring where Thomas tied the donkey when Simeon first arrived, he touched it with affection and walked down toward the river past the graveyard and up the hill on the other side. He spent the rest of the day praying on the Mount of Olives across the Jordan before going to the priest.

Rachel wept bitterly. Seth and Irad tried to console her, but to no avail. She rushed to her father's house to find Aiko and Jared waiting for her. She went directly to her mother's arms, began weeping loudly and then looked at Jared with fire in her eyes. "He went to you first, didn't he?" Jared nodded yes. "Why? I am his wife, I am the one who loved him at night and shared my life with him. I am the one he has always trusted. Why does he now turn to *you*?"

Jared remained silent. He knew she felt cheated and betrayed. All he could do was to reach out to her and Aiko, gather them both in his arms and weep with them. They stood there in grievous weeping until finally, in exhaustion, Rachel dropped to the floor and sat in the corner by herself in a stupor.

Late that afternoon, Simeon began the walk to the priest's quarters at the top of the hill. He went the longest way he knew and slipped in the door as so many before him had done. The priest sat there in the dimly lit room on a high, throne-like chair and greeted Simeon. "What brings you here my son?"

"I fear the worst. I have come for you to pass judgment on my ailment. I have no other place to go," Simeon answered. He stepped forward to the chair and the priest stopped him about two meters from the chair.

"Where do you want me to look, Simeon?" For the priest knew the greatest master potter in all of Jerusalem. Sadness filled the priest's eyes, as he looked upon yet another poor soul destined for obscurity and sure death.

"Here on my head," answered Simeon as he removed the cloth on his head. The priest stood on the platform of the chair and bent forward to look at the spot of missing hair on Simeon's head. More hair had fallen since Simeon had shown Jared. The priest took a small stick; much like the one Jared had used, and parted the hair. Small pieces of skin fell to Simeon's shoulder as before. The smell was strong enough and familiar enough that the priest didn't even need to bend closer to sniff it. He stepped back and threw the stick into the fire.

"Your fears are confirmed, Simeon. I am sorry. But let me talk to you."

Simeon's legs became limp and lost their strength, and he dropped to the hard tile floor. A groan came from his body as he leaned forward and began to rock back and forth.

"Simeon, listen to me. It is important that you understand what I am about to tell you. You must leave your clothes here to be burned. Put them into the fire over there. Then put on the torn garment that I am about to give you. Consider it your uniform. I will give you a small bell that you must wear around your neck at all times and warn others of your arrival wherever you go. Do you understand?"

"Yes, I understand," whispered Simeon as he raised his head and looked the priest into his eyes and then he asked, "Is there anything I can do to be cured? There must be *something*!"

"Only a prophet can cure you now, and it has been eight-hundred years since anyone has been cured. Unless you know a true prophet of Yahweh, there is no cure."

Simeon slowly rose to his feet and ceremoniously removed his clothing and tossed them gently into the fire with his headdress. He slipped on the tattered robe and the priest handed him the bell on a small leather necklace. He pictured the old basket weaver in his mind and remembered thinking that this was worse than death itself. Then he asked, "Do I have to go down the hill past my shop like the others? I want to spare my wife, Rachel, the pain of seeing me this way?"

"No. Then, you will have to walk through town and it will be very unpleasant. The people hate it. Do you know where to go?"

Simeon realized that he knew nothing of where the lepers went. He never knew of a leper.

"You must go to the colony in the caves. They are on the west bank north of here. Here are instructions. I suggest you spend as little time as possible deep in the camp because the community moves the worse ones deeper into the caves, where they die and are ultimately burned. Food is scarce. Do you have any with you?"

"No."

"That is too bad. Here is some bread from the temple for you. It will only last a week. Gentile children bring food to the colony. Very few of them contract the disease for some reason so they will bring you food. It is a hard life, Simeon. I wish you good fortune. Now you must go."

Simeon turned and looked out the door. A silent terror filled his heart, and he dreaded faceing the people. Nevertheless, he knew he must. Others before him had to do it and so could he. He exited and immediately turned toward town and walked briskly and boldly nearly shouting "unclean!" as he moved through the town. He didn't look anyone in the eyes and didn't let his eyes search for anyone he knew because customers would surely see him and gasp. All he could think of was that he would never see Rachel again.

As he approached the colony, he remembered John. Perhaps he did know a prophet. *Was the one crying in the wilderness really what he said he was? I must find him again.* He turned and didn't enter the colony, but started toward the Jordan River and headed southeast. He would find him or die.

Chapter 27

Enoch studied hard and knew as much as any priest in any synagogue concerning the coming Messiah. Unlike the priests, he had a purpose beyond political power and popularity. He now knew the Messiah was born in Bethlehem and was a contemporary but had no idea what he would look like. He still wanted the Romans out of his life and if the Messiah was alive, Enoch was going to be a part of his army.

The next morning Enoch approached the fishing boat as usual. He kept quiet about the Messiah since he was sure the others would scoff. He even avoided mentioning it to Nathan. Instead, he asked if anyone knew of any recent prophet in Judea.

"There is one called John the Baptizer who teaches along to Jordan," one of the men replied.

"Yes, I have heard about him too," responded another. "He teaches repentance and attacks Herod and his henchmen."

Enoch decided to share what he had found. "The Messiah will be born in my home town, the City of David. Bethlehem. He was the child the soldiers were trying to kill when they killed my younger brother, David. The Messiah will be the age of my dead brother."

They looked at him in astonishment and wondered if he had gone mad with all this study. "Well, John is about the right age. He preaches repentance, but that is about all we know."

Enoch laid the net he was mending on his lap and thought for a moment. *I need to get to Galilee. I will not find the Messiah sitting here in Alexandria. This is my sign to move back.* "I am going back to Galilee! Can we fish northeast of here tomorrow? You can let me off somewhere, and I can travel the rest of the way by land,"

"Just like that, you are going to leave us? Do you really think this prophet is the Messiah? No, Enoch. You come back with us to unload the catch, and then you can be on your way!"

Enoch knew better than to argue with them. The next day he fished and helped unload. He said goodbye to Nathan and his mother and headed out that very night. He had rations and money in his pocket, and he knew he could make it back to Galilee again, on foot if he had to. Now, taking a ship seemed the logical choice.

Enoch knew the ships and their destinations, which made it easy for him to hitch a ride with those he knew. He left Alexandria with his meager belongings and never looked back for he knew his brother was in Jerusalem and that he could stay with him for a little while. He no longer feared the Romans because too much time had passed, and he was just a small fish in the ocean of terrorists who had appeared in the last few years. Surely, the soldiers had moved on to other, more urgent missions. He arrived in Jerusalem two weeks later.

As he entered the town, he went straight to the temple and worshiped there. Then, as he left the temple, he asked about a potter called Simeon of Bethlehem. The first person he asked knew where the shop was located and sent him to the street that sloped down the hill toward the valley. Enoch had a mission, and he was intent on finding two things, his brother and John the prophet. He certainly knew his brother and would soon know if John was the Messiah.

Enoch looked about halfway down the second hilly street and saw a downcast young woman seated on the street with pottery all around her. He approached her and asked, "Would this be the shop of Simeon, son of Jacob from Bethlehem?" he asked.

Rachel looked up. "Yes. Would you like to buy one of his pieces, kind sir?"

"Actually I am looking to talk to Simeon. I have not seen him in years. I am from Bethlehem too, and I knew him as a boy. Is he in?"

Rachel's eyes returned to the pottery surrounding her. "I have a special price for you then. Are you sure you are not interested in a piece?"

A little irritated at the woman, Enoch insisted, "I want to speak to Simeon. Is he in?"

Irad come out from the shop and spoke to Enoch. "No, Simeon is not in right now. Can I help you?"

"Yes," Enoch replied as he raised his arms and ceremonially stepped around the useless woman. "I am Simeon's brother, Enoch, and I would like to wait for my brother's return if it is not too much trouble."

Rachel looked up again with renewed interest. "You are Enoch?"

Enoch ignored her for a moment, but when Irad deferred to her, he looked her in the eyes and knelt down to be on the same level. "Yes. I have come to Jerusalem to see my brother and his family. Do you know when he will return?"

Rachel quickly rose to her feet. She motioned for him to follow her into the shop. Enoch looked at Irad and Irad nodded that he should follow the woman. As he entered the shop, he noticed a partially finished piece on the wheel and that the fire in the kiln was only a flickering ember. Again, he asked, "When will my brother return?"

Rachel motioned for him to sit down on a bench along the wall, but Enoch remained standing. "We don't know where your brother is. He left a week ago. I doubt that he will be returning. I am his wife, Rachel."

"He spoke of you when we met in Alexandria, Rachel. What is wrong? Why would my brother leave his shop and family?"

Irad spoke the words that Rachel avoided. "He has leprosy, Enoch. The priest diagnosed him just before he left. We have no idea where he has gone and I doubt that he will ever return. We will lose the shop as soon as the word spreads that he has leprosy. Some customers have already stopped coming here and some even destroyed his pieces. They are easy to identify by his mark. People are terrified of leprosy here in the city."

"And with good reason I might add!" Enoch replied. "You have no idea where he is? Surely he is in a colony nearby."

"No, I have gone there to find him. I thought he may be hiding there, but they assured me that he never appeared. I fear for him," Rachel said.

"I do too," Irad added.

"We must find him!" Enoch said. "I will check the colony again. Maybe he will speak to me if he is there. I must find my brother. It has been too long since we have spoken, and he needs to know that I am back in the region. I will take care of him if I need to. I owe him much since I have not been the brother that I should have been. Our family is shattered because of me, and I must repay my debt to him. I am sorry, Rachel. I didn't know who you were. And you sir, who are you?"

"I am Irad. I worked for your brother. Seth, another worker, has moved on to another shop. I could not find work, so I am still here. Sit and I will get you something to drink. We need to talk."

Enoch sat down and placed his belongings on the floor. Rachel left the room so Irad and Enoch could talk alone. She sat on her mat and began to cry quietly. Then she laid down in the corner in the fetal position and quietly went to sleep.

Irad spoke first. "Simeon left Rachel some pottery he made and it sold for a few days, but now we have no income. I slept here a few nights to keep an eye on things, but eventually I had to go back to my wife and family. She is lonely and very upset. Forgive her for being so distant. She and Simeon were very close. She spends most of the day sitting outside and sometimes scrapes gold from a piece Simeon found in Alexandria. It has helped support her but it is nearly gone. Her parents are getting old and they don't have much. I don't know what will become of her."

"I am a fisherman and obviously can't work here. I have no home anywhere. I came only to say hello to my brother. I hoped to find John, the prophet who baptizes, before going on to Galilee. Now, I don't know what to do."

"Can you stay?" asked Irad.

"I don't believe I can. I need to make a living by fishing. I used to live in Bethsaida and know people there who will let me fish with them. As Simeon's brother, I feel like I must take care of Rachel, but I never figured on that. I know nothing about being a husband, and honestly, it never sounded very good to me."

"I am not sure she would leave the room in the shop that Simeon made for her. She is deeply devoted to Simeon, and I think she believes he will somehow return," Irad explained. "I don't know what is best for her, but she can't stay here forever. Perhaps you could come back for her when it makes sense."

Enoch thought for a moment. "I need to find John the Baptizer. I can come back for her if John is not who I hope he is. Otherwise, I will be occupied in a way that prevents me from taking care of Rachel. Is there anyone else who could take care of her?"

"Well, there is Nadab," replied Irad. "But I do not trust him. He has lust in his eyes, not love. I have no work and must move on myself. Seth is not going to take her in either. We talked about it. It is a mess, Enoch. Nevertheless, take a few days and see what you can learn about this John. Then please come back, either way. We will try to work something out with Rachel's parents. They are good people and perhaps can help with some money or something. In the meantime, we will sell what we can to pilgrims who come to Jerusalem. They are the only ones who will buy, and the others keep quiet about the leprosy."

"Thanks, Irad. I will say goodbye to Rachel and be on my way." Enoch went to the curtain and called to Rachel. Since she didn't answer, Irad and Enoch peeked in. She was asleep on the mat in the corner. Enoch knelt down, touched her sleeve and said, "Rachel, I will be back. Stay here for awhile, will you?" She nodded without opening her eyes. The men went outside, said their goodbyes and Enoch set out to find John.

Chapter 28

Simeon had nothing to eat. Desperate to find John, he pushed on and located the Fortress of Machaerus where Marcus had imprisoned John, but had no way to approach. A young boy, obviously a Gentile from the light hair and accent, asked Simeon what he was doing. Simeon knew immediately that the boy knew nothing of leprosy or he would not have approached him. "I am trying to get a message to one of the prisoners," Simeon told him.

"You have come to the right place, my friend! For a meager fee, I will communicate with any prisoner you want," the boy responded with the voice of an experienced sales clerk.

I could have used this one in my shop. "Do you know John the prophet who baptizes?"

"Sure I know them all, and I can manipulate the guards to allow me to talk to anyone. They are bored, poorly paid and sick of being here. The only problem is that prisoners die every day, and I cannot guarantee that this prophet is still alive. I will talk to him for you in exchange for the bell and something I can use to bribe the guards."

"The bell? Oh no! I can't part with the bell!"

"Well what else do you have?"

Simeon thought for a moment. "I have a shop in Jerusalem. I could get you some pottery."

"Is it good stuff?" asked the boy.

"It is the very best."

"Okay, Jerusalem is a long way, but I have been there before," replied the boy. "Now, what do you want to know?"

"I want to know how to cure leprosy. It is just that simple," Simeon said. "Also, ask if he or anyone can cure it?"

"Okay, I will be back." The boy disappeared in a flash running toward the prison. He spoke to one of the guards, and the guard led him in. In a few minutes, he was back but didn't look happy.

"First he said to repent. I told him I had questions for him and he shut up. Then I asked him about curing leprosy. He said he didn't know how to cure leprosy, but the one who comes after him is capable of anything. I asked who this would be and he said, Jesus of Nazareth."

"Where is this Jesus," asked Simeon.

"Before I tell you, you must promise. I need two pieces of pottery, one for me to sell and one for the guard. Is it a deal?" asked the boy.

"It is a deal," said Simeon with a smile on his face. "It is a good bargain."

"Okay," he said. "John said that the one who is greater than he will come to Jerusalem and you will know it when he comes. We can go to Jerusalem together. You can give me the pottery then."

"Just one thing," Simeon said. "What is your name?"

"They call me Little Jacob. Actually, I don't know my given name. The Jews call me that as a joke."

"Jacob is a good name. My father's name was Jacob. My name is Simeon." Simeon reached out then withdrew, remembering that he must not be touched. "Jacob, you must promise me that you will not ask to be carried or anything. I am not to be touched. Understand?"

"Sure, I follow instructions well, that is how I survive. Now what do you have to eat?"

"Nothing, I have come all the way from Jerusalem and have eaten all I brought with me."

"Well, we need some food if we're traveling back to Jerusalem. Let me see…I think I know where I can get some. I keep a stash of dried fish and bread. I have been hording it for a week. If I bring you some food, do you promise to give me another piece of pottery from Jerusalem?" Jacob looked up at Simeon to secure a promise.

"Okay, it is now three pieces of pottery for your services," Simeon promised.

Simeon sat on the ground as Jacob ran north along the river. He was back in a half hour with a cloth filled with bread. Although in pieces, it was more than a loaf. Jacob offered Simeon a piece, and it was delicious but a little stale. "Not bad for a week old," commented Simeon.

"It was once quite good," replied Jacob with a smile.

"Well, let's get going to Jerusalem," urged Simeon. "I will get you your pottery as soon as we're in Jerusalem."

They both started northwest, back toward Jerusalem… the boy and the leper. Simeon worried about Jacob catching something, but Jacob never touched him or his clothing and as people approached, Simeon rang his bell and people would pass by leaving plenty of room. He avoided saying "leper" for fear it would cause the boy to question his own judgment and eventually abandon him. Both wondered who this Jesus was.

After traveling a couple of kilometers, a lone traveler with only a few belongings approached them from the west. The setting sun was behind him, and Simeon and Jacob could not see his face clearly, but he could see them very clearly. As the man approached, Simeon took hold of the leather strap with the bell and began to ring it. The man stopped in his tracks and held up his hand for them to stop.

"So this is where you escaped to, Simeon," began the man. "Your wife is worried about you, and your shop is failing. Why are you wandering around in the countryside?"

Simeon didn't know what to say, and Jacob was about to make a run for it when Simeon spoke. "Enoch, is that you?" Simeon's heart leapt in his chest. Could this really be true? He had longed for his brother for many nights even before the diagnosis.

"Yes, Simeon, it is your old brother. I have been looking for you. Who is your companion?"

"This is Little Jacob. I met him outside of the prison, and he helped me communicate with John, the prophet who baptizes," replied Simeon, as he stood stiff, wanting to embrace his brother, but dared not.

"Jacob, I am Simeon's brother, Enoch. I have come to find my brother and the same John." Then, turning to Simeon, Enoch asked, "Why did *you* seek John?"

"I hoped to find a cure. John sent me to Jesus of Nazareth. I owe Little Jacob, here, for his services. He is a good boy and gave me food and is coming with me to the shop for payment in pottery, my only wealth," Simeon explained. "And you?"

"Come, let us sit down and talk awhile. The road is empty today and we can talk," suggested Enoch. They all hiked up the hill a short way and sat on half-buried boulders in the shade of some overhanging fig trees. "I am looking for John because I hoped he would be the Messiah. If he is, I am willing to join his army to defeat the Romans. You can understand that, Simeon."

"So the hate is still strong in your heart, Enoch. Why not let it go? It will eat your heart away. I should know. It took Thomas a long time to teach me to let go of it. Now I am being eaten alive by leprosy. There is no justice, Enoch."

"Perhaps you are right, but I need to do something. I will not waste my life fishing. Our brothers are persecuted every day. We need the Messiah, Simeon. I hope it is John."

"I don't believe it is John. He is in prison and sent me to Jesus. I know he spoke of one who would come after him as being greater. Perhaps Jesus is our answer. You need a savior, and I need a healer."Do you want to turn around and return to Jerusalem with me or go on to the prison?" asked Simeon.

"I don't know," answered Enoch ,shaking his head in frustration. "Nothing is going as I planned. You have leprosy. John is not the Messiah. Rachel has no one to take care of her. What chaos!"

With the mention of Rachel, Simeon's eyes fell to the ground. Sorrow welled up inside of him, and he could hardly hold back the tears. Simeon looked up and Enoch could see the tears coming.

"I am sorry, Enoch. I believe our only hope is Jesus. If he *is* the Messiah, he will know what to do. I don't even know if he will bother with us and our petty problems, but we must try."

All this time, Little Jacob just sat there listening to the two brothers and wondered if he would be better off without these two. Yet, he wanted to know about Jesus too. His friends were impressed beyond measure, but he never went with them to hear Jesus. John was a good preacher, but he was imprisoned. If Simeon were not so kind to him, he would leave immediately, but somehow Simeon seemed like a good man. Little Jacob wanted someone to cling to, yet Simeon was untouchable. *Perhaps because of the leprosy, he thought.* Even so, he liked Simeon.

Enoch stood and brushed the dust off his garment. "We might as well head for Jerusalem. Not much use in just sitting here, I can't even fish," he joked. "What about you and Little Jacob? They won't let you stay in town. Can you find your way back here from Jerusalem, Jacob?"

"Yes, no problem."

"Okay, let's go." Enoch took the lead toward Jerusalem, and it was nightfall before they reached the edge of town. Enoch told Simeon to take the bell off, put it in his pocket and walk between him and Jacob. They sneaked into town, past the priest's quarters and went straight to the shop. No one was there. Irad had gone home and Rachel was next door with her parents.

Simeon was devastated to see the shop in such disarray, yet he understood. It was clear that the shop would not make it without him. "I need to talk to Rachel," Simeon announced.

"There is no way you are going to wake that family only to let them see you like this, Simeon. You would scare them to death and Rachel would be so upset she would never sleep again. If you want to see her, it will have to be in the morning. Stay here for the night," Enoch said.

Simeon was easily convinced.

Little Jacob plopped down on Rachel's mat and was out like a snuffed candle. Enoch and Simeon sat up most of the night talking about Nathan and Esther in Alexandria. Simeon was pleased that they were doing well but sorrowful to be reminded that he would never see his mother again.

Finally, Simeon reclined in a corner by the kiln to take the chill off the night air and quickly fell asleep. Enoch hardly slept. His mind raced from visions of Egyptian fishing boats to the small vessels used on the sea in Galilee. He pictured Romans surrendering to a mighty Jewish army led by a great prophet, greater than Moses.

Early the next morning, Enoch woke to the sound of footsteps approaching the shop. He looked up just in time to see Rachel shuffle into the shop. She was startled to see Enoch and spotted Little Jacob asleep on her mat.

"Have you found your prophet?" she asked, addressing Enoch but looking at Little Jacob.

Enoch smiled, "Better than that! I found your husband and my brother."

Rachel's eyes widened as she looked around. She still didn't see Simeon behind the kiln. Simeon rose and moved into sight standing silently as Rachel faced him from across the dusty room. He looked bad. The leprosy now disfigured his face. He was recognizable, but not the handsome man she married. She wanted to run to him but knew better.

Finally, Simeon spoke in a quiet whisper. "Rachel, my love, are you well? The shop is in shambles. Where are the others?"

"Simeon, where have you been? We were so worried about you. There was no news of your whereabouts."

"I couldn't face going to the colony. I pursued John the prophet who baptizes, hoping he could free me of this curse. He is not the one, but the one who can has arrived. Have you heard of Jesus?"

Rachel was listening with her heart. She didn't care about prophets, John or Jesus. She just wanted Simeon by her side again. "You can stay here! I will hide you!"

"No, Rachel. Not like this. I cannot transfer my curse to you also. Besides, I will be dead in a short while. I must find Jesus soon. Enoch will help me. On the way here, we learned that Jesus is preaching in Galilee. Enoch knows Galilee well, and he will take me there. We will soon know if Jesus is the one. Stay here until you hear from me. I will send word back with Little Jacob," he said as he glanced at the boy. "Prepare three, no four, pieces of pottery for Jacob to pay him for his service. He is a good boy worthy of his pay."

Rachel knew Simeon was a man with a mind of his own and even she could not change it. She reached out to him and in return, he reached out to her. Their fingers nearly touched as they held their hands out, palms up, to each other like two children unsure of each other. It somehow brought comfort and assurance. Rachel promised her heart that she would remain until she heard from Little Jacob or Simeon returned. Words were not necessary.

Simeon turned to Enoch and said with enthusiasm, "Let us begin our journey!"

Enoch and Little Jacob picked up their meager belongings and set out. Simeon glanced back at Rachel with a look of assurance and then he disappeared, once more, from her life.

The journey to Galilee was uneventful although they received many wary looks as people wondered what these two were doing traveling with a leper. Upon reaching the hills outside of Capernaum, Enoch questioned travelers from Syria about Jesus of Nazareth.

A young man spoke up. "He is traveling the hills and sometimes preaches from a hillside or by the sea, so that many can hear him. He speaks with authority, like no other man we have ever heard. Many have come from Decapolis and Syria, like us, to hear him. Stay on this road, and you will eventually meet with his followers. They are everywhere!"

Sure enough, the young man was right. Only two kilometers down the road, over the next hill, was a large group of men, women and children following one lone man up a hill. The man stopped at the top of the hill, turned to them and began to speak.

"I must get closer," Enoch said to Simeon and Little Jacob. "Simeon, there is no way you can join the crowd. They will recognize you as a leper, and you will ruin everything. Let me go forward and listen while you wait here. Little Jacob, do you want to come with me or stay here?"

"I will come with you. Will you be alright, Simeon?"

"Yes, I will circle around and wait there by the tree on the knoll behind the crowd. You can come for me later and let me know what he says," Simeon replied.

Enoch and Jacob climbed half way up the hill to where they could hear Jesus speak. His voice was clear and easily understood. Enoch even recognized the Galilean accent. He held everyone's attention, and the crowd was quiet. Even the children were listening as Jesus spoke phrases one would never hear from the priests. He spoke of things beyond the Law of Moses, something Enoch was looking for. *Yes, this could be the man. He speaks with such authority and truth. He understands the wickedness of the priests and Pharisees, but he speaks of marriage, making peace with your brother and being a light to the world. He even speaks of things we don't see or hear and speaks of righteousness. This may be the one! He could lead an army!*

Little Jacob on the other hand, heard of love for one another and saw a gentle man. *This is the kind of man*

I would like for a father....understanding and a man of wisdom and pure virtue.

Simeon stood by the tree for a short time and then awkwardly lowered himself onto a rock in the shade. He could not hear any of Jesus' words and dared not come closer.

Then, as if the world stood still, the breeze blew onto his face and the crowd blurred. Jesus' face became clear, even from such a distance. Jesus was healing the sick! Simeon could identify people from Syria, Jerusalem, and East of the Jordan. There were people in great pain, paralyzed children and even the demon possessed. Jesus was simply speaking, and his word alone healed them, but Simeon noticed that there were no lepers in sight. And no wonder! The crowd would scatter if one approached, just as Enoch said. Jesus spoke to them.

No matter how hard Simeon strained, he could not hear. He rose from his place in the shade and leaned forward to hear. His heart leapt in his chest as he heard the crowd gasp at the miracles and praise God. There before him was his savior. Simeon was convinced that Jesus could heal him too, if only he would.

Although Jesus continued to speak, Simeon only heard the crowd celebrating. He could not take his eyes off Jesus, as Simeon stood there captivated by the man.

It's him! I know it is! He is the one that John identified. I believe this man can do anything.

Soon Jesus was finished speaking, and although many followed him as he moved back down the hill, Enoch and Jacob circled around to the hill where Simeon was just rising from the rock by the tree.

Little Jacob spoke first, "Wow! The man knows what he is talking about. He must know everything there is to know. No wonder everyone wants to follow him. He is great! Did you see him heal those who were with him, Simeon?"

Before Simeon could speak, Enoch broke in, "I don't know," he said. "He didn't even mention the Romans. Why? They are our enemies."

"Oh really!" Simeon said, "Are not we ourselves our own worst enemies? I don't know about you, but the Romans are the least of *my* worries. They will come and go. Maybe not in my lifetime, but they will disappear just like every other kingdom. Nevertheless, the kingdom of God will be with us forever. I agree with Little Jacob, this is 'The One,' and unless he heals me, this cursed illness will kill me."

"So now, what is next?" asked Enoch.

"I will ask him to cure me! I believe he can with no problem at all. You saw what he did for those on the hill.

They say he has cured others. I have seen it myself, and I believe what I see. I will do whatever he tells me to do. I suggest you do the same, Enoch."

"Well, I want to see more before I believe," countered Enoch. "We need to find a place to rest. How about staying somewhere in these hills where no one will see that you are a leper. Little Jacob, are you with us?" asked Enoch.

"It sounds okay with me," replied Little Jacob.

"I don't want him to get too far away. I am going to follow him," Simeon said.

"You can't do that! They will prevent a leper from getting near him. They may even stone you."

"I have to go. I have no choice." With that, Simeon hurried toward Jesus and the crowd.

Little Jacob looked at both brothers and decided to stay with Enoch. He also believed that Jesus could do it and wanted to see it with his own eyes, but knew he could not keep up with Simeon. Enoch reluctantly pursued shaking his head as if Simeon were crazy as he followed him with Little Jacob in tow.

Within a few minutes, Simeon spotted Jesus in the midst of the crowd about to head out in a boat. The crowed looked at Simeon as he rang his tiny bell and said "leper" as he approached the lake. Oh, how he hated that bell.

The crowd separated and turned from him as he approached. They kept a distance of four of five meters as he came closer to Jesus and the edge of the water. Jesus never moved. He only stood there as Simeon approached. It seemed obvious that Jesus knew Simeon's intent.

Simeon could hardly speak. He knew Jesus *could* heal him, but didn't know if he was asking Jesus for something selfish. If so, Jesus may choose *not* to heal him. It was a chance he had to take. He thought of Rachel as he approached Jesus, and a pleading look came over Simeon's disfigured face as he knelt before Jesus. "Lord, if you are willing, you can make me clean,"[3]

Jesus looked Simeon in the eyes reached out, touched him and said, "I am willing, be clean."[4] Simeon could not believe Jesus would touch him! A feeling of warmth came over Simeon's body. Peace, as he had never experienced before, swept through his mind. His body relaxed and all angst was gone. Simeon knew God himself had touched him for only The Lord God Almighty had such power. Simeon whispered, "Jehovah-Rophe."

The crowd gasped with astonishment as Jesus removed his hand from Simeon's shoulder. Then Jesus spoke again, "See that you don't tell anyone. But go, show yourself to the priest and offer the gift Moses commanded, as a testimony

---

[3] Matthew 8:2, NIV
[4] Matthew 8:3, NIV

to them."⁵ Then Simeon rose, grasped Jesus and held him tight. He held on for a long time and finally realized that he must let go. He released Jesus from his grip and saw Jesus smile at him. Simeon turned and headed straight for Jerusalem throwing that terrible bell to the ground as he went, leaving Enoch and Little Jacob behind. He traveled through the night, startling many travelers in the dark. He was a man with a mission.

Enoch and Little Jacob looked all over for Simeon. Finally, they had to ask someone if they knew where Simeon had gone. "Have you seen a leper traveling alone who may have approached Jesus?" Enoch asked a young man.

"Yes! Jesus healed a leper, just minutes ago, right down there on the bank by the lake. It was fantastic!"

"What are you saying? Jesus healed a leper. Where is he now? Did you see which way he went?"

"He went to see the priest. Jesus told him to see the priest and he lit out of here like an arrow. Toward Jerusalem, I imagine."

Enoch looked down at Little Jacob. "Do you think it was my brother?" he asked.

Little Jacob smiled and replied, "Of course. It is just what Simeon wanted. Jesus actually chose to heal him." Little Jacob had mixed emotions and wondered if he

⁵ Matthew 8:4, NIV

would lose his new friend and perhaps his wages. "I think we need to follow him, Enoch."

"I agree, let's head toward Jerusalem ourselves. It will be daybreak before he can see a priest. I have no idea where he would go? The temple I suppose."

"We can ask someone at the temple or ask his wife."

"*No*, we won't bother Rachel with this too. She has been through enough already. We will go to the temple and ask."

Enoch and Little Jacob headed toward Jerusalem with the few belongings Enoch carried with him from Alexandria, a burden becoming more and more troublesome. Soon it was nightfall and neither liked traveling at night, but they were both so spirited that neither one would admit he wanted to stop. They too traveled through the night.

In the morning, they bought some food with the little money Enoch carried. They asked the baker if he knew of the priest that people saw after being healed of leprosy and he just laughed and reminded them that such an assignment would be dull work.

After eating, Enoch and Jacob headed to the temple. There was always someone there, so finding people was not difficult, but finding an answer was not so easy. As they approached the temple wall, a temple guard stopped Little Jacob. "You! There! You cannot enter." It was too obvious that Little Jacob was not a Jew. Little Jacob frowned and sat on the steps outside the gate with the other outcasts. Enoch had visited the temple only three days earlier, and the guard even recognized him. He left Little Jacob with an assuring nod that he would be back.

Once inside the outer wall, Enoch approached a young Levite and asked, "Where can we find the priest who sees lepers that have been healed?"

"I really don't know who that would be. I suppose the one who declared the leper unclean. Let me ask my friends, they might know."

The Levite disappeared, leaving Enoch standing in the outer courtyard. Enoch was uneasy and fidgeting. Time was critical.

"The one who declares a leper clean is the same priest who declared the leper unclean," replied the older Levite. "But it is not that easy you know. One must…"

Enoch cut him off, "And who declares a leper unclean in this town? There are so many priests."

"There is only one. His name is Samuel and he resides just south of the temple in a small workplace just before one descends a steep hill with shops."

"Can one of you lead me there?"

Both Levites looked at each other and wondered what kind of scoundrel this was. Neither was going to follow him outside the temple only to be assaulted. "No. You must find it yourself. Now be gone with you," said the oldest.

Enoch was happy to leave the place. He exited the same gate that he had entered and picked up Little Jacob. Neither was comfortable with the crowd around the temple. As they walked down the steps, they petitioned a passerby, "Where can we find the priest, Samuel, who has a workplace at the top of the hill just south of here?"

"Go around to the south wall of the temple and you will see three streets going down the hill. The second street is the one you want. His place is just at the top of the hill to your right as you start down. Simeon's old pottery shop is half way down the hill, you can't miss it."

"He is going there," Enoch said. "Then he will go straight to Rachel. They apparently are great lovers. Let's go find Simeon!"

They quickly rounded the temple and counted the streets. Sure enough, it was the same street as the shop. There was the priest's workplace on the right with a man sitting outside on a bench with his feet in a trickle of water running down the street, apparently washing his feet. The clothes were tattered just like Simeon's but they could not see his face. A small dog approached the man, and he patted the dog with great affection.

Enoch slowly approached the man. Then Simeon looked up. The face stunned Enoch, and he stepped back.

There was a grown man with the face of a child! His skin was as clear as a baby's skin, without a blemish. He looked just like he did when he was a boy!

Simeon spoke first, "Well brother, what do you see? Is my face as clear as the rest of my body? My feet don't even have calluses. My hands are smooth and my arms are without blemish. But my face, I cannot see!"

"You are…well…perfect! I can see no wrinkles or spots on your face. It is like you were born again, brother!" Enoch dropped his load, lifted his brother and hugged him until Simeon could hardly breathe. Little Jacob just stood there looking on in awe.

"Why are you sitting here, brother?" asked Enoch.

"Samuel is not here. He has not yet arrived. No one passing by will talk to me, and I don't know when he is coming. I must see him. It was Jesus' order."

"Jesus healed you then? What did he do?"

"I cannot tell you. I am forbidden to tell of the miracle."

"Well it doesn't matter. Everyone in Galilee knows about it. They were thrilled to tell us. They could hardly contain themselves. That is how we knew to come to Jerusalem."

Just as Enoch finished, Samuel came around the corner with a couple of new tattered shirts. Samuel recognized Simeon's clothing at once but could not understand why someone was just sitting there in tattered clothes. "What is this?" he asked.

"I have come to you so you can declare me clean. I am Simeon the potter."

Samuel looked at Simeon with a confused look on his face. "It can't be. I sent Simeon away a few weeks ago, and he would be quite bad by now. You cannot be him, yet you *do* look like him. You are not supposed to reenter the town once you are unclean." There was a long pause. "Well, come inside. You two …stay outside."

Inside, Samuel began questioning Simeon. "So, you say you are Simeon? What was your occupation?"

"A potter."

"What is your wife's name?"

"Rachel."

"What are her parents' names?"

"Aiko and Jared."

"Who had the shop before yourself?"

"Thomas."

"And what did Thomas do before he was a potter?"

"He taught in the temple."

The interrogation stopped. Samuel looked at Simeon and said, "Well if you are Simeon and I declare you clean and you are clean, then no harm. If you are clean but not Simeon, I see no harm either. Rachel will certainly know the difference. We must go outside of the city. You should not have come into Jerusalem."

Samuel took Simeon outside and approached Enoch. "Meet me later in the day on the hillside across the Jordan overlooking the city, you know, just outside the olive grove. We will be there for a long while. Simeon, you will not see your friends until I am finished."

While they waited, Enoch went to Jared's house. After the customary greetings, Enoch sat down and said to Jared, "I have seen my brother and he is well."

Jared assumed he meant that Simeon was in the leper camp and doing well. "Well, the poor boy needs someone to visit him. I am not sure I should tell Rachel, however. She is really struggling with the shop, and I wonder what will become of her once I pass away. I am getting old and don't have many years left, you know."

Enoch knew that Jared was hinting that he take over Rachel and look after her. Enoch played along and said, "I will gladly watch Rachel. But I have no place and no talent, except fishing, and fishing is not a suitable occupation here in Jerusalem."

Jared sighed and looked down. "If it means Rachel will have to leave it may be best." Jared was not enjoying this conversation at all.

"I really need to clean up after my long trip, and then I will return and perhaps we can think of a better solution, given a little time to think." Enoch seemed strangely happy and excited about the idea.

Jared was not so sure about this young stranger.

Later, as Enoch walked the path to the olive grove, Little Jacob met him on the path. "Enoch, Samuel has asked Simeon to shave his whole body, even his eyebrows. He looks really strange!"

Enoch was irate. He hiked down the dusty path to the Jordan and up the hill toward the "garden", as it was called. When Enoch saw Simeon standing there naked and shaved all over, he insisted, "What on earth is this all about? Why have you humiliated my brother like this?"

The older Samuel looked Enoch straight in the eyes and replied, "It is the law of Moses, young man."

What could Enoch say? He looked at Simeon with concern. Simeon just smiled back and shrugged his bare shoulders. Simeon didn't care. He was so happy he was cured and being shaved mattered little to him, and besides, he knew his hair would grow back.

After the examination, Samuel declared, "You are not only clean, but you are without blemish, young man. I should keep you here for weeks, but I have sick to see and things to do at the temple. Why you insist you are Simeon, I will never know. Put on your clothes and go."

"One question if I may," asked Simeon.

"And what is it?"

"What is it that Moses says I must sacrifice?"

"It is a lengthy procedure and requires sacrifice on your part. You don't appear to be a wealthy man, so we shall use the less expensive procedure. I will order two birds, cedar wood, scarlet yarn and hyssop from the temple for you. I will kill one bird and then dip the other bird in the blood of the dead bird along with the wood, yarn and hyssop.

I will then sprinkle blood on you seven times, pronounce you clean and release the live bird. You can go home but must not go *into* your home. You must sit outside, where everyone can see you and not hide. Then on the seventh day, you must shave again, just as you have just shaven, and bathe. On the eighth day, you must bring a lamb for a guilt offering to the temple along with a small lamp of oil and an ephod of finely ground grain. I will take the blood of the lamb and oil and anoint you. The grain is for a grain offering. Then you must sacrifice two doves for a sin offering. Then you will have fulfilled Moses' law."[6]

"I must do exactly as you instruct me," replied Simeon. "Let it begin."

With that, Simeon washed in the Jordan and put on the new clothes that Enoch gave him. He walked back to Jerusalem with Samuel, Little Jacob and Enoch. They

[6] Reference

239

went directly to the temple and Enoch bought the lamb, birds and doves. It nearly wiped Enoch out.

After entering the temple, Samuel killed one bird, dipped the other into the blood of the first along with the wood, hyssop and yarn. He sprinkled the blood, mixed with oil, on Simeon. By this time a crowd had gathered to see what was going on. Some even recognized Simeon and Samuel was embarrassed that he didn't believe Simeon at first. Finally, one of the regular customers asked Simeon how he was cured of such a dreaded disease.

Simeon just stood there without answering. Enoch spoke up, "Jesus of Nazareth healed him in Galilee."

Samuel stiffened and could not hide the terror in his eyes. He had been a part of Jesus' work! *What will the other priests say if they learn this? Yet, it is true. I have seen it with my own eyes. Only the grace of God could make a man so flawless.* Samuel told Simeon to go home and sit outside the shop for seven days and follow his instructions.

Simeon walked with his brother and Little Jacob down the hill to the shop. Tears began to well in Simeon's eyes. Most who travel down this hill from the priest's shop feel doomed and despised as a leper. He felt freedom and joy, the same warmness that he felt when Jesus first touched him. He was unaware of the crowd following him until he reached the pottery shop.

As Simeon approached the shop, Rachel walked out of the door wiping the dust from a pitcher with a cloth. She looked up at the commotion, and her eyes went directly to Simeon's clean, flawless face. There was that face that Rachel loved so much, the intense, bright, brown eyes of her beloved Simeon.

Rachel dropped the cloth and pitcher in delight. She immediately knew who he was! She ran up the hill into his arms and embraced him in sobs. "Oh Simeon, my love, you are here with me again. How can this be?"

"Jesus of Nazareth sent me home to you, Rachel. By the mercy of God, I am a clean man, fit for such a lovely lady."

Those around the couple began to praise God and sob with joy along with Rachel. Never had they seen such a thing, such joy and happiness, such a miracle. Shop owners from the street came to greet Simeon and welcome him home. Simeon stood with his arm around Rachel and greeted them, and when they asked about his healing, Enoch always chimed in and explained everything to them, in great detail even though he had not seen it himself.

Little Jacob just stood nearby, dumbfounded by it all.

Pilate and Herod were not getting along. Not a good sign for either, but especially for Pilate. You only get one chance to be a Roman Governor of a province.

Chapter 29

"Simeon! Jesus is coming to Jerusalem! Everyone in town is talking about it!"

"At last! I knew he would come sooner or later," Simeon responded. He shared Rachel's excitement at the idea of Jesus arriving in Jerusalem.

"Exactly when do people think Jesus will arrive?" asked Simeon.

"Today around noon I believe! We need to greet him, Simeon. Do you think he will remember you?"

"I suspect so. He caught a lot of criticism for the miracle, if you can believe it. I think the stiff-necked people of this town will give him a hard time too. They just fail to understand his teachings, and he is not what they expect.

He is kind and unlike our cruel kings. I can hardly wait for you to hear him speak, Rachel. You will love him."

"I love him already for giving me you," she replied and then gave Simeon a big hug while not upsetting the piece he was making on the wheel.

"Let's tell the others. They will be excited too."

Rachel left the front of the store and scurried inside. Little Jacob was stacking pots on the lower shelves since they were the only ones he could reach. Enoch was sitting by the kiln and watching the fire with Irad.

"Come with us outside, I have good news. we're about to close!"

"What about the fire?"

"It will wait for this!" Rachel and Simeon said in unison as they exited the front of the shop.

Once outside, they all gathered around Rachel. She explained, "Everyone in town knows that Jesus is nearby and headed for Jerusalem. We figure he will be here about noon. Simeon and I want to greet him as he arrives, and I think we should all go together. How about it?"

Simeon told them, "Stop your work and let the pieces go. They matter little. Then we can go to the edge of town to meet Jesus as he approaches."

Everyone smiled except Enoch who still never smiled. He looked troubled instead of expressing delight. Jesus' patience with everyone was a real problem for him since he wanted a liberator so badly and still hated the Romans with a fire that Simeon could not extinguish.

As mid-day approached, everyone in the shop was ready to go except Rachel who was always last. She wanted to look her best when she met Jesus, her husband's redeemer. They finally left and the men were anxious to get to the edge of town in time to see Jesus approach. When they arrived, they were surprised to find a whole entourage of people waiting and eagerly looking down the narrow road.

It was hard to see over all the people, and poor Little Jacob could see nothing but the backs of those in front of him. As noon approached, Simeon hoisted Little Jacob onto his shoulders, and when he tired, he switched with Enoch. Rachel moved forward so she could see well as she stood among the women. In anticipation of the "King's" arrival, many of the women pulled palm leaves and distributed them among the children.

After about an hour of waiting, the crowd could see a man on a small white donkey coming toward town with men following close behind. Nearly everyone was sure it was Jesus. Some were surprised he was on a donkey, but others understood the symbol of a king coming in peace.

As he approached, the people began to chant. "Hosanna! Hosanna in the Highest! Hosanna, son of David!" They called him many names depending on their experiences or what they knew of him. Simeon wanted to shout Jehovah-Shammah, but dared not utter the words. The women and children began to lay the palm leaves on the ground in front of the donkey as they bowed in greetings. The crowd was so excited that it permeated the air like a fine perfume. Crowds never greeted anyone in such a way. Not even royalty.

As Jesus moved into town, the throng could not follow him because the streets were too narrow. It was obvious he headed for the temple, but Simeon and the others took a longer, less crowded path to the temple. They talked with anticipation as they scrambled to beat the pack. Everyone that is, except Enoch who lagged behind and was strangely quiet.

Once they arrived at the temple, they could see Jesus stroll among the tables where the moneychangers sat and where the Levites sold the doves and lambs. Then, without warning, Jesus challenged one of the moneychangers who had just cheated a young, out-of-town couple. The moneychanger just sneered at Jesus and told him to mind his own business. That was all Jesus could abide! He grabbed a rope from the canopy of a nearby booth and handled it like a whip sending the moneychanger scrambling for cover. Then he overturned the table and the coins flew into the air like startled quail. The other moneychangers headed for cover as Jesus shouted, "It is written that my house is to be called a house of prayer, but you are making it a den of robbers!"[7]

He turned to the benches where they sold doves and lambs for sacrifice and overturned them too. Anger raged in his eyes, somehow, he knew they were reselling previously rejected offerings as acceptable, blemish-free offerings to unsuspecting out-of-towners.

Enoch was delighted. Finally, he saw the Jesus he expected, one with authority and knowledge, one who would challenge the status quo. Yes. *This* was his man!

Simeon on the other hand, was frightened speechless. Jesus had unexpectedly shown anger and malice toward the authorities. Never in his wildest dreams did Simeon think he would do such a thing. But, here it was. Simeon agreed with Jesus, but somehow was shocked that Jesus would be so bold.

Rachel cheered with many of the other women. She knew that they cheated women the most, and she hated it. She had gone to the temple to offer sacrifices while Simeon was sick, and *every time* she went, they cheated her. What could she do? But now, Jesus was setting them straight, and she tasted sweet revenge!

[7] Matthew 21:13, NIV

Little Jacob was astonished. *These Jews are certainly an emotional lot.*

Irad didn't know what to think. He saw it but could not believe anyone would do such a thing.... even if it were right.

The commotion brought the Chief Priest and the teachers of the law out into the courtyard. They arrived just in time to see the blind and lame, often cheated by the moneychangers, approach Jesus and ask for healing. He gladly complied and taught as he healed. Everyone was excited and thrilled at the miracles and authority of Jesus. All, that is, except the Chief Priest and his teachers of the law. They were white-hot with anger.

Suddenly some young children, caught up in the excitement, began to chant the same thing they had heard their parents say earlier in the day. "Hosanna to the Son of David!"

When he heard this, the Chief Priest said to Jesus, "Do you hear what these children are saying?"[8] He expected Jesus to rebuke the children.

Jesus simply replied, "Yes. Have you never read, 'from the lips of children and infants you have ordained praise?'"[8] The pompous Chief Priest and his hooligans were stunned into silence.

---

[8] Matthew 21:16, NIV

Then, Jesus turned and left the temple and traveled to Bethany to spend the night with friends. The small band from the pottery shop began their short walk home, and Simeon asked, "What bothers you, Enoch?"

"I don't know. I guess it bothers me that Jesus came into town the way he did. I expected a more stately entry. He is the 'King of the Jews', you know."

"How can you say that, Enoch? He is *The King*, born in the linage of David, a humble man, performing many miracles, including mine! The others hate him because he preaches a new kind of law in a new kind of kingdom, not one of strictly 'an eye for an eye', but one of mercy and grace. We need to change, Enoch. We Jews are nothing as God intended us to be. Sometimes I am ashamed to be a Jew. I think we are missing the point."

"I do too, Simeon, but I don't know what 'the point' is any longer. What is salvation after all? Is it salvation from the Romans or our own corrupt leaders? This country is a mess! Young people don't even know scripture."

"Well, if you remember, *we* didn't know much either. You had a rabbi to teach you in Alexandria, and I had Thomas. We are blessed. Thomas taught me that the Messiah would be a peaceful man, but you look for one of war. I don't really know which is right either."

"That is why I am troubled, Simeon. I just don't know."

"We will see, Enoch. We will see. Time has a way of sorting these things out."

The next day was work as usual. Rachel was out front, and the others were inside making production. Sales were a little better since strangers were in town because of Passover and the arrival of Jesus. He had a regular following that was surprisingly large. They were people from all over and all occupations. Even a tax collector was among the twelve who were his closest friends.

Suddenly, a friend of Enoch's came to the shop all out of breath. His name was Cleopas. "Where is Enoch? He has done it again! He has struck!"

"What did he do?" asked Rachel as Cleopas hurried past her and proceeded into the shop as if he had been there many times.

Rachel followed.

Spotting Enoch, Cleopas shouted, "Enoch, he struck today. The priests and elders were outraged, and he just faced them down. He was wonderful, Enoch. Wonderful!"

Enoch looked delighted. He looked at Simeon as if to ask if he could go. Simeon nodded approval, and Enoch flew out of there with Cleopas. As they raced toward the temple, Cleopas explained, between breaths, that Jesus entered the temple again and was met by the Chief Priest and the elders, and they asked him by what authority he did the things he did.

"He was great, Enoch! Jesus said to them, 'I will also ask you one question. If you answer me, I will tell you by what authority I am doing these things. John's baptism-where did it come from? Was it from heaven, or from men?'[9] It was great; they just stood there, speechless. Finally, they said, 'We don't know.'[10] Jesus said he wouldn't answer them if they wouldn't answer his question. Then he taught in parables. The embarrassed Chief Priest left, and then the Pharisees tried to trap him, but they couldn't either. Wow! Jesus is amazing!"

As Cleopas and Enoch entered the temple, they could hear Jesus teaching. He was hard to see, but it didn't matter. His voice alone had more authority than the temple itself.

Jesus taught the crowd. "The teachers of the law and the Pharisees sit in Moses' seat. So you must obey them and do everything they tell you. But do not do what they do, for they do not practice what they preach. They tie up heavy loads and put them on men's shoulders, but they themselves are not willing to lift a finger to move them.

"Everything they do is done for men to see: They make their phylacteries wide and the tassels on their garments long; they love the place of honor at banquets and the most

---

[9] Matthew 21:24-25, NIV
[10] Matthew 21:27, NIV

important seats in the synagogues; they love to be greeted in the marketplaces and to have men call them 'Rabbi.'

"But you are not to be called 'Rabbi,' for you have only one Master and you are all brothers. And do not call anyone on earth 'father,' for you have one Father, and he is in heaven. Nor are you to be called 'teacher,' for you have one Teacher, the Christ. The greatest among you will be your servant. For whoever exalts himself will be humbled, and whoever humbles himself will be exalted.

"Woe to you, teachers of the law and Pharisees, you hypocrites! You shut the kingdom of heaven in men's faces. You yourselves do not enter, nor will you let those enter who are trying to.

"Woe to you, teachers of the law and Pharisees, you hypocrites! You travel over land and sea to win a single convert, and when he becomes one, you make him twice as much a son of hell as you are.

"Woe to you, blind guides! You say, 'If anyone swears by the temple, it means nothing; but if anyone swears by the gold of the temple, he is bound by his oath.' You blind fools! Which is greater: the gold, or the temple that makes the gold sacred? You also say, 'If anyone swears by the altar, it means nothing; but if anyone swears by the gift on it, he is bound by his oath.' You blind men! Which is greater: the gift, or the altar that makes the gift sacred? Therefore, he who swears by the altar swears by it and by everything on it. And he who swears by the temple swears by it and by the one who dwells in it. And he who swears by heaven swears by God's throne and by the one who sits on it.

"Woe to you, teachers of the law and Pharisees, you hypocrites! You give a tenth of your spices--mint, dill and cummin. But you have neglected the more important matters of the law - justice, mercy and faithfulness. You should have practiced the latter, without neglecting the former. You blind guides! You strain out a gnat but swallow a camel.

"Woe to you, teachers of the law and Pharisees, you hypocrites! You clean the outside of the cup and dish, but inside they are full of greed and self-indulgence. Blind Pharisee! First clean the inside of the cup and dish, and then the outside also will be clean.

"Woe to you, teachers of the law and Pharisees, you hypocrites! You are like whitewashed tombs, which look beautiful on the outside but on the inside, are full of dead men's bones and everything unclean. In the same way, on the outside you appear to people as righteous but on the inside you are full of hypocrisy and wickedness.

"Woe to you, teachers of the law and Pharisees, you hypocrites! You build tombs for the prophets and decorate the graves of the righteous. And you say, 'If we had lived in the days of our forefathers, we would not have taken part with them in shedding the blood of the prophets.' So you testify against yourselves that you are the descendants of those who murdered the prophets. Fill up, then, the measure of the sin of your forefathers!

"You snakes! You brood of vipers! How will you escape being condemned to hell? Therefore I am sending you prophets and wise men and teachers. Some of them you will kill and crucify; others you will flog in your synagogues and pursue from town to town. And so upon you will come all the righteous blood that has been shed on earth, from the blood of righteous Abel to the blood of Zechariah son of Berekiah, whom you murdered between the temple and the altar. I tell you the truth; all this will come upon this generation.

"O Jerusalem, Jerusalem, you who kill the prophets and stone those sent to you, how often I have longed to gather your children together, as a hen gathers her chicks under her wings, but you were not willing. Look, your house is left to you desolate. For I tell you, you will not see me again until you say, 'Blessed is he who comes in the name of the Lord.'"[11]

Jesus then turned and left. Again, the leaders in the temple were speechless. Enoch noticed Nadab among those standing there. Nadab was speechless too. Enoch wanted to say something to him but dared not, since Nadab had just been insulted with the rest of his cronies.

---

[11] Matthew 23:2-39, NIV

Chapter 30

Nadab was furious. *How could he say such things about us and claim to be a prophet?* Nadab knew that the others were plotting to get rid of Jesus somehow, but he had no idea what they had in mind.

Finally, the Chief Priest called Nadab to a counsel in the chamber of the Sanhedrin. As he called them to order, the meeting room became quiet. The Chief Priest addressed the assembly. "I know that this Jesus has been an annoyance to our work here. I am sure his popularity will pass. See to it that the man is no longer among us at the Passover. I don't want him on the streets, understand?"

After his brief statement, he left and the Sanhedrin, faced with selecting a group to see to it that the Romans arrest Jesus before Passover.

Fortunately for Nadab, he was not selected as one who would plot Jesus' arrest. He left the assembly dejected and confused. He wondered what charge they would select since all Jesus had done was to insult them. Yes, it was awful, but it was not unlawful. Nadab was a *law* abiding Pharisee, and it didn't seem logical that the Romans would arrest Jesus. After all, the Romans insulted the Jews every day. He would just have to watch this unfold.

It was well known that Simeon was a follower of Jesus, and eventually he got news of the Sanhedrin trying to trap Jesus. They had every opportunity in the temple every day, but could not approach Jesus because of his popular teaching and followers. After much self-debate, Simeon mustered enough nerve to ask Nadab what was going on. He met him at a shop where they served lunch and bought lunch for Nadab. Then Simeon asked, "Nadab, what do you think of Jesus?"

Nadab knew that Jesus supposedly cured Simeon of his leprosy, but Nadab figured it was a natural cure and not a miracle. He was careful to be politically correct in his reply, "He has done some great things for the people, but I don't think he is a genuine prophet. He is too hard on the faith to be a real Jew. Why not be hard on the Romans? After all, they are the enemy, not us."

Then Simeon asked his real question. "Do you think he is the Messiah?"

"Oh! Heavens no! He offends God. He is a rebel of some sort. The Messiah will rebel against the Romans, not against us Jews!"

"Are you sure, Nadab? I see wisdom in his preaching. I see honesty and truth."

"You would, Simeon. You cannot be objective. He cured you! It is one thing to claim to be a prophet and try to correct the corrupt practices in the temple, but it is entirely another thing to be the Messiah. No. He is *not* the Messiah."

"Enoch wonders also. He is expecting a warrior."

"Good for Enoch."

"Be careful, Nadab. This is important stuff and you are in a position to be sure Jesus is given an honest chance."

"You be careful too, Simeon, that you are objective and not swayed by the miraculous. I believe some of these things are tricks."

Simeon rose to his feet, looked Nadab in the eyes and scowled, "You are just like the other stiff-necked scoundrels in the Sanhedrin!" then turned and left.

Simeon was more confused than ever. How could someone like Jesus be so kind and honest and generous and yet be an enemy? He still believed deeply that Jesus was the Messiah. Nothing was going to change that.

Nadab was confused too. Yet he was angry with his naïve friend. Nadab was not convinced that Jesus was really the Messiah and was not going to believe easily. He knew that others had fooled many naïve believers only to leave them bitterly disappointed and even dead.

Chapter 31

"Get out of there, Simeon. You and Enoch need to quit snitching samples. The Passover meal is too serious a thing for you two to be picking at the food all the time. Passover is two days away, and you can at least wait until the food is cooked!"

Rachel was busy preparing for the feast. All of Jerusalem was in great turmoil about Jesus, and the temple priests and teachers of the law were outraged.

"I love the tension in the city that Jesus has created. People are thinking again and not just following the rituals," Simeon offered with no prompting.

"Well, I agree," Enoch chimed in. "At least we agree on something. I know it will be a long time before we know the truth, but the debate is great."

Little Jacob just took it all in like a sponge and had formed his own opinion but didn't share it with anyone.

Jesus continued to teach in the temple. More people than ever were convinced that Jesus was genuinely the Messiah. Those who expected a warrior were emboldened and spoke often of overthrowing the Romans. Yet Jesus continued to address eternal issues, never challenging the Roman authority even when prodded to do so.

Word spread that Jesus would often meet with his disciples at night in the very garden where Simeon and Rachel had their picnics. Little Jacob spoke-up and said, "I would like to know this Jesus better, and I know he is going up on the hill across the Jordan River at the end of the day. Some of his followers go along just to be close to him and hear what he and his closest followers have to say. May I go tonight after I have finished my chores?" he asked.

Rachel said, "I don't like the idea, and it may be dangerous."

However, Simeon stopped her before she could say no. "You may go, but you must be home shortly after sundown, and we will expect you for supper. Understand?"

"Yes sir," said Little Jacob, a remarkable response for such an independent gentile.

Little Jacob crossed the Jordan, walked by the graveyard along the path and climbed the hill following rather closely behind the others. He heard many discussions about the "Kingdom of God," something he had never heard of before. It was late when they arrived in the garden, and there were only a few other followers except "the twelve" and not even all of them were there. He talked to a few of them, but they were tired and didn't respond well to his questions. Eventually, Little Jacob sat down as close to Jesus as he thought he could without being sent away by one of the twelve.

Jesus seemed upset and went off to a place out of sight to pray. Little Jacob knew enough to respect Jesus' need for privacy and sat on the ground to wait for his return. Then he fell asleep.

Suddenly, Little Jacob woke with a fright, as the light from hundreds of torches seemed to bring daylight to the garden. The sounds of shouting Roman soldiers, temple guards and terrified followers filled the air. Jacob rose to his feet just as a Roman soldier was taking Jesus by the arm. Jacob rushed forward toward a young soldier to protest. Just before he reached the soldier, another soldier grabbed his shirt, probably saving his life. Jacob twisted and turned until the soldier finally released him, but Jesus and his custodians were well out of reach.

Little Jacob ran the whole way home ducking and turning whenever a soldier was nearby. He entered the city and crouched as he moved from shadow to shadow. Finally, he sprinted up the last few yards to the shop and ducked inside sobbing and struggling for breath. Rachel was reclining in the bedroom with Simeon and heard him plop onto the floor gasping for air. She jumped to her feet and rushed into the shop with Simeon close behind.

Between sobs, Jacob recounted the incident. Rachel was outraged. "How could they do such a thing, and in the middle of the night? What kind of animals are they? They twist his every word; they slander him in the temple; they treat his followers like dirt and now this!"

Simeon had never seen Rachel so furious. He held her a while to calm her down. "Settle down, nothing will happen till morning, and then we will see what happens. They can't possible hold him long," he told her. "He's done nothing wrong."

She glared at Little Jacob as if she were his mother, but she was so happy he was safe that she just stooped and lifted him to his feet and pointed him to his mat. "I will talk to you in the morning, young man!"

Enoch slept through the whole thing.

Chapter 32

The next morning when Enoch woke, everyone else was awake and in the worst of moods. He asked, "What is the matter? Everyone seems upset. Did I miss something last night?"

Rachel replied before anyone could get a word in, "Yes! Those stinking Romans arrested Jesus last night."

"What! Oh no! Has anyone seen Cleopas?"

No one answered.

"He was with Jesus last night! He's a great follower and a friend of Simon, the one Jesus calls Peter, one of the twelve. Simon used to fish the same waters that I did. I've known him for years. Simon, not the one they now call Peter, was even a Zealot! They may have arrested him too. Oh, I must go!" Enoch yelled back over his shoulder as he flew out the door.

Enoch raced up the hill. *Where can I find them? They must be somewhere in town. If I were them, I would certainly be hard to find.*

Enoch went to the temple first, but the temple was a bad idea. People were everywhere because of the feast. The temple cashiers were doing their usual bilking of the out-of-towners, and temple guards were apparently on alert. There was no way the disciples would be there for fear of more trouble.

After rushing out of the temple, Enoch stopped for a moment and looked around for anyone he knew. There, among the shadows of a fruit stand, stood Cleopas with his back to the crowd. Cleopas slowly turned and glanced back over his shoulder at Enoch in recognition. His eyes were glassy and nervous from being up all night and darted as he searched the crowd for soldiers.

Enoch approached the fruit stand and began inspecting a basket of dates. Without looking up, he whispered, "Follow me." He turned around and began walking toward the pottery shop hoping that Cleopas was close behind. At the intersection above the shop, Enoch stopped and turned around. There was Cleopas following closely. Enoch handed him his cloak with a hood, and Cleopas silently put it on, raised the hood and walked beside Enoch. Neither man said a word.

Enoch considered the danger Cleopas may pose and though it unwise to go into the shop. He stopped again in front of the basket shop and asked, "Do you think we are being followed?"

"I don't think so; since I was arrested last night and then released. They only seemed to want Jesus and were not interested in the rest of us. The Temple Guards are who took him. I followed him all over Jerusalem last night. They tried and convicted him in a matter of hours. I don't think they care about me. we're safe."

Enoch said, "Let's go into the shop then. Come with me."

Once inside, Cleopas became very animated. "He is in prison. Jesus is in prison and the temple leaders want him crucified! The Roman soldiers don't care one way or the other."

"What! How can that be? They just arrested him last night. There hasn't been a chance for a trial," Simeon replied in disbelief.

"Simon, the Zealot, and I were arrested and then let go. Apparently, the soldiers only wanted Jesus. The temple guards took him all over town to rush it through. None of us could stop them because we feared for our lives. He was arrested for some trumped-up charge that I don't understand, something akin to treason."

"Treason! The Romans think he has committed treason? What kind of fools are they?" Simeon was hot!

"The Sanhedrin did this," Enoch said with disgust in his voice.

Simeon asked, "What can we do? He is no traitor. He never disparaged the Romans. He took them for what they are, our captors. We need to go into town and talk to someone."

"But who?" asked Enoch, with an angry look on his face.

"Nadab," Simeon replied.

Simeon looked at Rachel. "Rachel, you know Nadab. Would he do such a thing?"

"I don't think so, Simeon."

"You're probably right. He is a teacher of the law. He loves the law, and this is contrary to the law. Come with us, Rachel, and help us convince Nadab to help Jesus if he can."

"I will go with you, but Nadab is just one of many and not very high up," replied Rachel.

All of them rushed up the hill toward the temple, except Cleopas who was too afraid and exhausted to go. When they arrived, some of the people were there weeping for Jesus. The healed blind man and a few others were outraged and bold in their anger. A number of men argued that it was only right that he be off the street by Passover. They claimed he was a menace and needed locking up.

Simeon entered the temple and asked, "Where is Nadab, the teacher of the law?" A temple lackey pointed to a set of stairs nearby. There was Nadab in his finest with tassels swinging as he descended the stairs like a noble. Simeon stomped over to the foot of the stairs and stood with his hands on his hips as if to challenge Nadab. "What is going on Nadab?"

"What do you mean?" asked Nadab with feigned innocence.

"Come with me Nadab we need to talk," commanded Simeon. They both passed through the gateway into the crowded outer courtyard to meet Rachel and the others. When Nadab saw the angry look on Rachel's face, he became visibly upset and defensive. "Gamaliel and Samuel spoke-up and tried to reason with them, but the ones assigned to get Jesus off of the street were set against him," Nadab stammered. Then Nadab lied, "I tried to reason with them too, but they wouldn't listen. Honestly, I did."

Simeon didn't believe Nadab but kept quiet for Rachel's sake.

" Why crucifixion, Nadab?" he challenged.

"That is the penalty for treason."

"What treason, Nadab?"

"Claiming to be 'King of the Jews'"

Simeon knew this phrase to be one the people used, not Jesus. Suddenly, he also realized that the people had sentenced him with their words. Simeon fell silent, as did the others.

"There is nothing you can do," Nadab continued. "He is in the hands of Rome."

Chapter 33

His beautiful wife was furious. Pilate sat in his chair pouting as she pleaded with him, cajoled him and tried to manipulate him. Actually, he loved it when she was like this until she finally said, "This is what you will be remembered for, Pontius; making the most outrageously stupid decision in all of history."

"Shut up, I don't want to hear any more of your ridiculous dreams. I was almost convinced God sent Jesus or was a ruler of another kingdom. Yet, there he stood in *my* custody. The Sanhedrin was on my back to do something and insisted on the ultimate charge.

"If he is indeed the 'King of the Jews' sent from God to straighten those idiots out, perhaps you are right. It would be stupid of me to do away with him. Let the Jews themselves decide what to do with their 'king'. It will not be *my* decision. It will be *theirs*. Now, shut up, I want to hear no more of it! Do you understand?"

"Yes." Her head bent in a gesture of exhaustion. "I just don't want his blood on *our* hands."

"I said; NO MORE!"

She turned and left the room in slow retreat. Her head ached and her body shuddered. She had grown to hate Palestine and now her relationship with Pontius was a hate-love relationship slowly turning more toward hate. She used to respect him, but now she saw a fear inside of him, a fear of the Jews and the Romans alike, and it made him weak. One offense and he would be gone from his post. At this point, it would be a blessing to her.

Pilate rose from his chair and paced the marble floor. He felt anger flow through every muscle of his body. He felt his heart pound and the blood rush inside of him. *Why is this so hard? I have sentenced others to the cross. Some were clearly guilty, and it was no problem for me. Others… well I was unsure. I guess the difference is that I am sure this man has not offended Rome. He is not guilty of anything worthy of crucifixion. What do I do? How can I live with myself if I sentence this man? I can only wash myself of his blood and let the Jews decide. If he has enough followers, they will want him released.* He sat back down. "Let his blood be on their hands," he said in a whisper.

Chapter 34

Nadab was reviewing an upcoming lesson when a temple lackey approached him. "Nadab, The High Priest wants to see you as soon as you can get there."

Nadab had met the High Priest before, of course, but now the High Priest called on *him*. Nadab felt honored. As he entered His Excellency's chamber, he was met by six others sitting quietly along the wall on the floor as if awaiting execution. Another teacher of the law greeted him with a nod, as Nadab joined his friend on the floor. The others looked him over but said nothing. It appeared to Nadab that they were from all occupations. One even looked and smelled like a fisherman. Another looked like he was perhaps a merchant, and yet another seemed to have real money, a Roman perhaps.

Then the Chief Priest entered the chamber with his usual flair. He began politely, "Thank you all for coming. I have brought you together for an assignment of the utmost importance." Then he paused to seat himself on an ornate chair, out of character for the otherwise bare room. He continued, "As you know, Jesus of Nazareth was arrested last night and is now in Rome's custody which is just where he belongs." Most nodded their heads at these remarks, but Nadab sat stiff and still… afraid to look around as the Chief Priest continued. "I am concerned about a legal loophole that may result in Jesus' release if we're not careful.

"It is Passover, and if Pilate feels like it, he can offer one prisoner to be set free as a token to the people in honor of Passover. He may or may not offer anyone. He may offer us a choice. I just cannot predict. Yet, we must not be complacent. We must NOT allow this man to set Jesus free on the Passover. He has done enough harm, and we cannot let his insolence continue. He will corrupt the people by his teachings, and I want all of you to help make sure justice is done.

"There are many people here in Jerusalem who feel the same as we do, that Jesus is a blasphemer, or at best a dangerous rebel, who must be silenced before he brings all of Rome down upon us. This is why we must assure ourselves that Rome deals appropriately with the injustice. Pilate is a weak man, and I believe he does not realize the seriousness of Jesus' threat. It takes Rome to exercise the justice required in this case. For that reason, I have brought you together to help the people of Jerusalem and all of Judea to force Pilate to crucify Jesus."

There was a long pause as the seven took in the seriousness of the punishment. Nadab dared not flinch.

"I have set aside some funds from the treasury to use to reward those who will simply shout for justice against Jesus. Each of you knows people in your circle of friends who will do this for nothing, but we need a large crowd. If you can locate aliens who will accept our thanks for watching and being ready if Pilate comes out to offer a release, then promise them whatever it takes. In this way, there will be no doubt in Pilates' mind that the people prefer crucifixion for Jesus. I will make sure that those in power know how Jesus has claimed to be a King of the Jews. Pilate will not survive letting Jesus go.

"Be sure the people chant 'Crucify him!' above any others who may speak. Do you all understand?" He gave a cold stare to each of the seven and no one so much as breathed. "Very well, as you leave, you will be given a portion of the money. Use it all, and use it wisely. I want you to enlist as many as possible to close this loophole."

The Chief Priest continued to give them instructions and extracted a promise from each that they would do their best. He also promised a reward for them if they succeeded.

273

After the meeting, he called Nadab aside and gave him special attention. "I know you would like to serve in the temple. I will reward you with this privilege if we succeed in crucifying Jesus. Nadab, I want you to do your best for our people. Nearly everyone likes you and you have much influence for your young age. Do we agree on this?"

Nadab was stunned. His closest friends would forsake him if they ever learned of this. Yet, it was his job to do as the Chief Priest said. He must not hesitate. "Yes, Your Excellency." He spoke with false conviction.

"Then go to it, my boy. Go to it."

Nadab exited with his head up high and chest out but inside he ached. *There is no room for fence-sitting on this issue. I am forced to decide. Why me? I wish it had been somebody else, but I have a duty, and it is right, of course. Who can I find to do this for us?*

Nadab talked to some of his friends, and the ones Rachel had not talked to were easy marks for the plan. They did not want anyone messing with their Jewish festivals and feasts. To them it was obvious that Jesus could not be the Messiah, since the Romans so easily arrested him. He didn't even have an army and had plenty of time to assemble one.

Others had talked to Rachel, and some had even heard Jesus speak. None of them, not one, would speak against Jesus under any circumstance. They said the charges were trumped, and justice would *not* be done if one hand were laid on this magnificent prophet. Nadab became more aware of the split in the people's thinking as he asked for help. It increasingly bothered him that not a single person who had heard Jesus or seen his miracles would speak against him.

That night Nadab fitfully dreamed of Jesus looking him in the eye accusingly. He saw Jesus reach out to him in his dream, and as Nadab withdrew, grab his tassels and rip them from his robe.

A man from Damascus discovered a dead man dangling from the end of a rope, an apparent suicide. No one knew his name, but a few recognized him as one of the followers of Jesus.

Chapter 35

Pilate ordered Marcus to have Jesus scourged immediately. "Turn him over to the detachment on duty, and allow them to do as they please," he said. "I need to show the people that I have indeed punished him severely."

Marcus took Jesus to the whipping chamber inside the palace so that it was not a public spectacle. Once inside he gave the familiar order with the stipulation that they are to stop short of killing the man.

The soldiers never questioned Marcus' orders, but they always drank themselves into a stupor before a crucifixion of a malcontent. The work had no glory, no reward, and no fulfillment. The assignment went to the detachment that was on duty that day. No rhyme or reason to it, just terrible dumb luck. Marcus hated it too. It reminded him of that night in Bethlehem with the mercenaries. They were drunk too. Marcus often tried to control his men's fierce resentment of the Jews and their assignment in Jerusalem where there were so many Zealots and religious fanatics, but to no avail.

Marcus was irate when he left their presence. *Why are we doing this to an innocent man at this time at all? Let them have their feast, or whatever, in peace. Why are we forced to such cruelty now*? Yet, he had no real control. Being a Centurion under Pilate had no real power. He was just a go-between, a puppet for the authorities, and he realized that it was his cruel reality. He was less a real leader than before. His men obeyed him well and even liked him, but there was no gratification in his assignment. It was a hollow, cruel existence.

The soldiers made great sport of this Jew claiming to be so important in a kingdom that, apparently, didn't exist. They pushed him, laughed at him and finally whipped him, as instructed, but could not stop there. The wine had taken their senses away. Cruelty became fun.

The thorn crown was an afterthought. With the thorn tree just outside, it made a convenient source of scorn. "King of the Jews" they called him and laughed as they pushed it down into his scalp.

By the time they were finished, Jesus was stripped and nearly dead. Yet, he only looked at them with a dignified resignation. He even seemed to understand their fierce resentment. Never did he lash-out at them in anger or plead for mercy. His response finally brought them out of their stupor, and they quit. If Marcus were present, he would surely have stopped them earlier. They put his robe back on but left the crown in place.

Marcus returned to the dark chamber and was horrified at what he saw. "Are you men out of your mind? You had better hope this man survives his beating, or you will get a chance to see what it feels like yourselves! Pilate wants him outside. Now get him up to Pilate!"

Once outside, Pilate looked at Jesus with approval. He planned to offer Jesus to the people, thus ridding himself of the awkward situation. Both Marcus and Pilate fully expected them to request Jesus once they saw the punishment for his offence.

Pilate turned to the crowd. He noticed strangers among the usual riffraff, Pharisees and Scribes along the edges of the crowd, and even some from the Sanhedrin. *This should be interesting. Will they save their own? Or, are they so jealous of Jesus that they cannot bear to see him survive?*

Pilate stood by Jesus, while Marcus stood by Barabbas, a notorious Zealot. Pilate looked out over the crowd and began his oration. "Here are two of your people. In honor of Passover, I give you the choice of which of these you would have me release. Which one do you want me to release to you: Barabbas or Jesus, who is called Christ?"[12]

Just then, Pilate's manservant brought a message to him. Pilate raised his hand to silence the crowd as he read. Surprisingly, they complied. It was from his wife, which read:

Don't have anything to do with that innocent man,
for I have suffered a great deal today in a dream
because of him.[13]

Pilate gazed at the letter. He could only hope the people would choose their "King" over this filthy killer.

Then he turned to the crowd and asked, "Which of the two do you want me to release to you?" [14]

"Barabbas," they answered.[14]

Pilate was shocked. *What is going on here?*

"What shall I do, then, with Jesus who is called Christ?"

They shouted all the louder, "Crucify him!"[15]

Pilate had to quiet the crowd to ask them, "Why, what crime has he committed?"[16]

---

[12] Matthew 27:17, NIV
[13] Matthew 27:19, NIV
[14] Matthew 27:21, NIV
[15] Matthew 27:22, NIV
[16] Matthew 27:23, NIV

The crowd would not stop. They kept shouting, "Crucify him! Crucify him! Crucify him!" Over and over they chanted in unison while drowning out the few who tried to shout for Jesus' release. Pilate could see men move through the crowd and silence the ones defending Jesus, and he could see he was getting nowhere by asking them repeatedly.

Then he turned from the crowd and asked his manservant for a bowl of water. The manservant quickly reappeared with the requested bowl and held it out ceremoniously as Pilate raised his hand to the crowd, insisting on silence. Then he dipped his hands deep into the bowl and began to wash his hands scrubbing them as if they were filthy. He remembered what his wife had told him the night before. He thought it would bring relief to disown the blood of this innocent man, but nothing seemed to ease his angst.

"I am innocent of this man's blood. It is your responsibility,"[17] he shouted in anger at the crowd.

"Let his blood be on us and our children,"[18] one of the hired protesters shouted in response.

Pilate turned to Marcus and ordered the release of Barabbas. Marcus was not pleased to release this killer into the hands of the crowd but reluctantly complied. Then Pilate, with head bowed, whispered the command

---

[17] Matthew 27:24, NIV
[18] Matthew 27:25. NIV

for Marcus to have Jesus prepared for the crucifixion. The words nearly choked Pilate who turned and entered the darkness of his chamber.

Since protesters kept taking the crosses down from Golgotha, the Soldiers kept crosses in the whipping chamber and made the criminals drag the crosses up the hill. Jesus was in no shape to carry his cross, so as they left, they grabbed a gawking spectator from out of town, and gave him the job, since he seemed strong enough and would not hold up their progress. Their thinking was certainly clearer now.

News of the mock trial and staged spectacle before Pilate's Judgment Seat had spread all over Jerusalem. Simeon closed the shop, and they all went into the streets to try to get a glimpse of Jesus and to see for themselves if it was true. They were shocked.

Jesus was nearly beat to death, and a few of the streets were speckled with mockers. Nevertheless, for the most part, the people were shocked into silence as Jesus passed by. Those who knew Jesus were either in tears or outraged. They knew that Jesus had not offended Rome but the Jewish leaders. Most knew that what he said about the leaders rang true, and knew he taught kindness and mercy not the cruelty that passed before them. This was clearly an unfit punishment for Jesus.

Rachel and Simeon felt lost and helpless. The soldiers were mean and angry as they kept the crowds back from the path. Simeon had to hold Rachel back even though he wanted to stop it somehow too. Simeon worried that they would come looking for his family someday just because he believed Jesus was indeed a king and the Messiah. The trip was grueling for the man dragging Jesus' cross. Everyone felt sorry for him too and wondered if he was a follower and this was his punishment.

Blood dripped from Jesus pierced brow and into his eyes. It oozed through his robe from the lashings on his back and ran down his leg. Simeon couldn't help but think back to that bloody night in Bethlehem. The soldiers were different, but the cruelty was the same. *How long will this go on? It won't go on forever.* He knew the blood would penetrate the pavement and last many rains, just as it did in the streets of Bethlehem. *Blood is not easily erased.*

As the procession reached the top of the hill, the soldiers laid out the crosses just as they always did. Three this time. They placed Jesus face-up on the middle cross and as two men held Jesus down, and another man held the spike, they pounded the iron through the hands and feet of Jesus. Jesus tossed his head from side to side in pain. The others cursed the Romans and struggled. Jesus still didn't curse Rome or threaten the soldiers but took it with bravery and with dignity as the soldiers lowered the cross into its hole with a thud.

The man who taught mercy never asked for mercy himself. This seemed strange to Simeon and Enoch. They looked at each other in wonder. How could he stand it!

The priests, elders and teachers of the law circled Jesus and mocked him. They hurled insults at him and defied him to get down from the cross if he was such a miracle worker. They were crueler than the soldiers were at this point. Even one of the robbers managed to get in his spiteful comments.

Simeon and Enoch told the women to return to the shop so they would not see any more of the horrible sight of the crucifixion. Rachel wanted to stay and pleaded with her almond eyes, but Simeon insistently nodded for her to go. She understood but wondered why men thought women could not handle such things. The other wives were relieved to be dismissed.

Enoch asked Simeon, "Do you think he *will* come down from the cross? You know, he performed other miracles. Why would he not get himself down and prove himself?"

"No, if the other miracles don't convince them, neither will this one. He did the miracles for others and not himself. There is no point in it. I think the willing, innocent suffering proves more than a miracle would at this point."

Simeon's reply prompted a deeper appreciation in Enoch. He knew that many prophets had suffered severe ridicule, and some, even torture and death. Daniel in the lions' den, and Shadrack in the fire were famous for survival, but he could see that Jesus was not going to survive this. *What does it mean?*

Marcus stood just a few feet from Enoch and Simeon, as he watched with horror as his men performed their terrible task. The men behaved the same way they did in Bethlehem, with detachment and barely controlling their own horror. He could tell they had numbed themselves with too much wine, but it was wearing off. The day was sunny and hot, and the crowd was unusually big. It was getting close to the sixth hour.

Marcus rolled his head back and gazed into the sky. It was getting very dark. In fact, suddenly it was *extremely* dark as if the sun had disappeared. He ordered fires, and a few of the men began building two fires, one in front of the crosses and one behind. The fires would keep the crowds back, and the soldiers could see what was going on. Marcus and the others wondered why it was getting dark at this time of day.

The crowd took its eyes off the crosses and looked up too. Some crouched and ducked as if some monster was going to get them. The darkness sank to the ground, pitch black in places, and the fires didn't seem to penetrate this unusual darkness. Marcus kept an eye on Jesus. He saw tears in Jesus' eyes as he spoke, an unusual phenomenon, because it was so hard for such a beaten man to get breath while suspended by both arms. Jesus would push himself up with his nail-pierced feet and shout.

Marcus could not always hear what Jesus said, but caught the phrase, "Forgive them for they don't know what they are doing."[19]

Marcus watched the tears mingle with the blood on Jesus' face. Finally, one dripped from his drooping head straight to the ground. When it reached the ground, Marcus felt the first tremor. The ground actually shook as Jesus' tears hit the ground. No one else seemed to notice, but Marcus did. Something was happening! Would this man actually come down from the cross somehow? Marcus was puzzled and finally realized that this was no ordinary man. He remembered Herod speaking of a "King of the Jews" when he commanded the Roman soldiers to enlist some mercenaries to kill the two-year-olds. Could this be the one? Marcus began to panic. *What have we done!* Then he whispered, "Surely this was a righteous man,"[20] just as Anthony walked up.

"What do we do with this crowd, Marcus? It is pitch-black up here."

---

[19] Luke 23:34, NIV
[20] Luke 23:47, NIV

"Send them away to their homes."

"A man has asked for Jesus' body to give it a decent burial. Should I allow it?"

"Yes, it makes sense."

"The Jewish leaders are protesting. They want the body guarded."

"Then guard the tomb, Anthony!" Marcus replied, with his eyes still fixed on Jesus face. He never even looked at Anthony. "And see to it that all three are dead before we disperse the crowd."

"Yes sir. I believe the center one is dead already."

"So do I, I heard him say, 'It is finished.'" Rather triumphantly, I might add."

With that, Anthony picked up a spear and broke the legs of the two robbers to prevent them from hoisting themselves up to gulp for air. They would suffocate in due time. Jesus seemed to be dead, so he pierced the side of Jesus just under the rib cage and blood and water flowed out indicating that he was indeed dead. Then he motioned to the man in the crowd to take the body. A couple of soldiers helped reluctantly as they seemed to have mercy on Jesus after all. Apparently, the wine was wearing off. They had to ask a group of other soldiers to move away from the foot of the cross. They were gambling for the blood-soaked robe Jesus left behind.

It was still horribly dark with shadows flickering from the fires. The scene was surreal. It was dark for three grueling hours.

Chapter 36

Nadab was nowhere near the hill. He was in the temple lighting incense before the veil separating the Holy of Holies from the rest of the temple. As he performed the familiar ritual, he stood with his head down and dejected. He felt betrayed by his own faith. All he could think about was the fact that Jesus was not guilty, killed for offending the priests, scribes, Pharisees and teachers of the law. Killed! It just didn't seem right to Nadab, but how else could they silence him.

Nadab looked up and whispered, "Oh Lord, what else could we do? Help me understand what is going on here. I don't know whether to celebrate or mourn. Jesus taught with such conviction and authority, and yet, what he taught would undo all our traditions and your system of laws."

Suddenly, the ground shook and Nadab tumbled into a sprawled heap on the floor of the temple. The light stands crashed to the floor, and all of them went out except one in the chamber and the one on the other side of the curtain. It was extremely dark everywhere else.

The earth continued to shake, and the walls swayed. Then the earth settled down, and Nadab rose again to his feet. He brushed his garment to shake off the dust. Then he looked up as he heard a tearing sound. Very slowly, almost imperceptibly at first, the curtain began to tear from the top at the center. Four other priests rushed in with torches in their hands to see what was happening and to relight the lamp stand. The veil tore completely from top to bottom revealing the Holy-of-Holies. Nadab and the others fell to their knees.

Nadab had his answer! God had left this place. It was no longer the holy dwelling place of God. God was offended and Nadab knew it. The others did too but stood there in disbelief. Nadab remembered the words of the man in the crowd, "Let his blood be on us and on our children." Nadab shuddered and wept.

Chapter 37

The soldiers shuffled Simeon and Enoch down the hill along with the others. The brothers walked side by side in silence. Simeon's healer was gone, and Enoch's hero was gone. Neither man wanted to talk. They were ill. The whole thing was so cruel and final. What hope did they have?

Finally, they reached the shop, and Rachel was inside trying to hold back her uncontrollable sobs. Simeon held her in his arms, close to his chest, and she seemed to melt in his arms. She looked up at him and, with tears in her eyes, asked, "Simeon what does this mean? I am confused. Help me understand."

Simeon had no answer. He only held her tighter. Finally, he replied, "We must wait and see. We simply need to wait."

"I was afraid of the dark. The whole world seemed to be in turmoil. The ground shook, and pottery fell from the shelves. I tried to save some but was terrified! I just sat on the ground and watched them fall. What will we do?"

"The pottery is unimportant now. We will simply make more. We have to go on somehow. It will be alright, Rachel. It'll be alright."

Little Jacob slowly walked from the doorway, where he was standing, toward the couple and stood next to Simeon. Simeon slowly parted from Rachel, reached down and brought Jacob into the embrace. Little Jacob was one of them now, no denying it. He understood Simeon and Rachel's devastation, and he needed them as much as they needed him.

Enoch walked over to the kiln, laid another log on the fire and poked at it mindlessly. Then he pushed the stone, used as a door, back in place and turned to look at the three. He longed for the companionship that Simeon and Rachel shared. He was tired of living all alone. Even his mother and Nathan were no substitute for a family of his own. Yet, Jesus never had a family either. Like Enoch, he seemed alone except for the followers who constantly surrounded him. Yet, he died as alone as any man he had ever known. *It could have been me hanging next to Jesus. I could have been one of them.* He walked over to the three, put his arm on his brother's shoulder and wept with him. Never had he felt as empty as now.

As Enoch looked over the shoulder of his brother, he saw a figure move in the back of the shop, dimly lit by the glow of the kiln. He raised his head and stiffened. Who is the elderly man in the back of the shop who seemed reluctant to show himself? He withdrew from the embrace, looked at Simeon, and nodded his head toward the figure. Simeon turned and saw what was bothering his brother.

There in the shadows, stood a familiar form that Simeon had seen in the same dim light before. The man slowly moved forward into the light of the shop. His clothes were rumpled and his face pale, but it was clearly Thomas! Then he spoke with the same soft, gently voice he had used so many times with Simeon when he was a boy.

"Simeon, my son, it is good to see you again."

"Thomas, how can this be?"

Rachel let out a sobbing squeal, put her hands on her mouth and retreated to the far wall, both terrified and bewildered. She then scurried back to Simeon's arms. At the same time, Jacob moved behind Simeon to a safer place.

"Don't fear Rachel," began Thomas, "I have indeed come from the grave. The stone rolled away when the ground shook, and I am now alive. I have seen the splendor of the Messiah, Simeon, and so have you. Today death was defeated, and life was given to those who believe."

Simeon didn't know what to say. He stood there motionless for a moment then he moved to Thomas and reached out his hand to touch him. Thomas stood with his arms open wide as Simeon touched his chest. Thomas slowly wrapped his arms around his adopted son and embraced him just as he had so many times before. Rachel then moved in as Thomas included her in his embrace.

Then Thomas spoke again, "I am here for only a short time, but you must know that I am real and not a figment of your imagination. The times have changed, my son, and you and the others must not leave the city. You, Enoch, and the others will see what the Lord has laid upon Jerusalem and this generation. A new day has dawned. The night is over. The serpent is crushed."

"What does he mean 'the serpent is crushed', Simeon?" asked Rachel.

"It means that mankind has found salvation, Rachel," Thomas answered. "Now I must go. But know that I love you and will see you on the other side." With that, Thomas turned and walked toward the door. Rachel called him back, but he didn't return. He walked out the door, and as they rushed out to see him off, he was nowhere. In fact, the street contained only a couple of unfamiliar pedestrians.

The four silently walked back into the shop. Stunned, none knew what to make of the experience. All agreed that they saw Thomas and heard the same news. The instruction to stay in the city seemed strange, and they agreed that it was impossible to stay the rest of their lives in the city. They decided there must be some event that they are to see or experience.

Enoch was the only one who still doubted the experience. This all seemed very mysterious to him, and he didn't know this Thomas. For all he knew it was an imposter. Confusion reigned in him. *What did Thomas mean by "salvation had arrived?"* He didn't sense any change. He didn't hear any army come and throw the Romans out of the city. In fact, when he looked out again, there was a soldier passing by just as they always did, with the same smirk on his face. No, it would take more than this to convince him that something had really changed.

That night, Simeon and Rachel could hardly sleep. When he did drift off, Simeon dreamed of weeping believers on their knees begging for mercy before Roman soldiers standing stiff and expressionless.

Rachel tossed and turned in her sleep while dreaming of Jesus struggling for each breath he took as he hung on the cross.

***

Jerusalem was not the same the next day; it was never the same. People would glance over their shoulder toward Golgotha, and their eyes would drop to the ground as their gaze turned back to the street. Even the merchants seemed subdued after such an event. All wondered if the day would somehow become dark as it had the day before. News of the torn curtain spread quickly throughout the city creating bewilderment regarding its meaning.

Simeon and Rachel sat among the remaining pottery without engaging any customers along the street. Most people knew that they were "believers" and didn't know whether to express consolation or boycott the store. Yet, they knew that this was the place to get the best and wanted to buy, so they just walked up and did business without mentioning the previous day's events. All, that is, except one, the gentile goldsmith from Macedonia named Justin.

"I have come to bring you some money," Justin greeted them with a smile. "I cheated you before, you see. The gold was more valuable than I told you. I have come to repay my debt to you."

Simeon stood silent as Rachel replied, "Justin, what has brought you here after so long?"

"I have a change of heart. After listening to Jesus of Nazareth, I am a changed man. Jesus convicted me to change my ways. What a powerful man he was! I never imagined myself as happy as I am now. Yet, since yesterday, I am confused. I should be overwhelmed with grief, but instead I am filled with new life. I'm now an honest man living among thieves and I love it. The freedom is tremendous!

"I knew of your healing at Jesus' hand and that is what brought me to the side of the hill where I listened to him speak. He was right, you know. We need to climb out of our rut of doing business without a heart and of following laws and traditions that hurt, more than help, our fellow man. He may be gone, but he has certainly left his mark."

Rachel and Simeon looked at the gentile and then at each other. He was right! Jesus may be gone but he has left his mark on everyone, even unbelievers. "Come into the shop, Justin, and sit with us for a while so we can talk. We need your encouragement," Simeon said.

"I must get back to my shop, Simeon, but I certainly will stop by tomorrow. I too need encouragement, and I need to know the meaning of this to you Jews."

"Come at noon, and we will break bread together, and perhaps we can figure out what it means to us Jews together, because I am not sure I can figure it out by myself. See you then?"

"Shalom Brother, I'll see you tomorrow."

Rachel looked at Simeon. "That was remarkable! He gave me this money. It is not much, but it is apparently, what I deserved. He walked here to deliver it and brought us the gift of encouragement. He seems like a nice man. What do you think?"

"I agree. It takes a lot of courage to admit to having cheated you, yet he seemed so glad to do it. Jesus did have a splendid effect on many of us, but I am surprised at how he influenced a gentile like Justin. Oh, how I wish Jesus was still here."

The next day, Justin showed up as promised. Rachel took over outside while Simeon, Enoch and Little Jacob sat down on benches and ate bread while discussing Jesus with Justin. Enoch said, "Isaiah, the prophet, seemed to say the most about one to come, but was Jesus the Messiah? That seems to be the real question. Yet, to die on a tree is the most horrible, defiling way to die and surely, the Messiah would not suffer such a humiliation in addition to dying at the hands of the Romans. The Messiah should overcome the Romans."

Justin was not so sure. "The Messiah was to come to the Jews. He was to change them and save them from something greater than the Romans. Yet, it seems inconceivable that he would die such a horrible death in such a brief time. Why did Jesus remain on the cross, when it was perfectly clear to many that he could do miracles?"

They had barely begun when they heard a knock on the door. It was Rachel with Cleopas and two women.

"The tomb is empty!" shouted Cleopas.

"What are you talking about?" Enoch retorted.

"Jesus' tomb is empty! Everyone is talking about it all over town. The guards were there at first, but now the Romans have taken them to their barracks to keep them quiet. John and the one they call Peter visited the grave and said that an angel announced to these two women that he had risen. What do you make of that, Enoch?"

"Who are you two?" asked Enoch, turning to the women.

"Don't you recognize me, Enoch? I am Mary, mother of James and John, wife of Zebedee. This is Joanna. We were there, Enoch. We saw it firsthand. Cleopas said you would not believe unless you saw for yourself. Come with us, and we will show you."

Enoch was stunned. He turned to Simeon and both rushed out the door nearly tripping over each other. They headed to the tomb, only a short distance away and found the gigantic stone rolled away from the door. Enoch paused at the entrance, a little afraid to look in, but Simeon said, "Go on in, nothing will hurt you."

They went in the tiny, dark space. Their eyes adjusted to the darkness, and there on the shelf that would normally hold a body, was a neat pile of burial clothes folded as if Jesus were to return to fetch them. There was no sign of a body! Enoch and Simeon backed out simultaneously and looked at each other, then looked at Rachel, huddled together with the other women. Simultaneous expressions of joy and bewilderment covered their faces resulting in an almost comical appearance.

"Lots of people have visited the site. It is empty all right," chimed in Rachel.

"Cleopas, do you know where the followers are now?" asked Simeon turning toward his brother's friend.

"No, they are not out and about for fear of the Romans," Cleopas said with a frown.

Simeon said, "Cleopas, you and Enoch go on home. I know Cleopas needs to make his delivery to Emmaus today. Rachel, Little Jacob, and I will try to figure this out before you return. When will you be back?"

"I should be back around noon tomorrow."

"Rachel, give Enoch some of the money Justin gave you, so he can pay for his food and lodging," Simeon ordered. Then, turning to Enoch, he said, "If this is true, it is a much greater miracle than coming down from the cross. Wouldn't you say?"

"Yes! I would certainly say so!" replied Enoch with wide eyes.

Enoch and Cleopas briskly set out for the shop. Simeon and the others lingered awhile and finally they too began to walk back to the shop while discussing the apparent resurrection.

Chapter 38

Mary and Joanna finally excused themselves and Simeon sat back down with Justin and Little Jacob while Rachel remained outside. "Well, what does it mean? If this is true, Jesus' power surpasses death. Could he be saving us from death itself? If so, what does that mean? There is something we are missing here."

"And is this gift for the gentiles as well as the Jews?" Justin wondered aloud.

Little Jacob finally spoke, "I hope it is forgiveness he comes to offer. We certainly need forgiveness. We all doubted Jesus at times. He *is* the Messiah and you are *still* debating it!" Little Jacob rose from the bench and angrily walked outside to be with Rachel. He loved her innocent belief, and she understood better than the men did! Rachel greeted him with a hug and held him close. He was as much her child as any boy could be. She knew Simeon felt the same. *He will be a great man someday.*

Inside, Simeon scratched his head and said, "The little gentile is right, you know. How much more do we need to know to believe? The tomb is empty, and the women are witnesses to the angel's message. Nevertheless, how will we ever know he has risen unless we see him ourselves, as we saw Thomas? Moreover, is it necessary for us to see to believe? I think not! I felt his power flow through my veins when he healed me. No person alive has that kind of power. It only comes from God."

"I agree," Justin replied as he rose from the bench. "We are brothers now, you and me. Time will fill in the gaps in our understanding. Shalom Brother, I will see you tomorrow." Then he left.

Chapter 39

Enoch and Cleopas gathered their personal effects in preparation for their trip. Cleopas grabbed the satchel of letters his employer had given him as they scurried out the door with a brief wave to the others. It was about a three-hour fast-paced walk for them to reach Emmaus, and Cleopas wanted to get there in time to deliver the letters to his contact before sunset. The satchel was relatively full since the day before was the Sabbath. Enoch, on the other hand, really had no business going to Emmaus, except to discuss the day's events with his close friend, Cleopas.

The road was wet from the previous day's rain, but easily traveled. Once on the road, the urgency seemed to seep from Cleopas, and he relaxed a little.

Cleopas began, "Let's see what we know about the Messiah anyway? I know that he should be a savior, but a savior from what? If you look at the sayings of the great prophets and our own history as a people, the Romans will come and go, like the Babylonians and others."

"Yes, and we know he should be born in Bethlehem, my hometown, and Jesus was actually born there. In fact, Herod killed my youngest brother while looking for a 'King of the Jews'. Could it be that Jesus somehow escaped the killings?" wondered Enoch.

Cleopas pulled his short beard, as was his habit. "Well, we know that Jesus grew up in Nazareth. Perhaps his parents escaped Bethlehem before the Romans killed the babies. How, on earth, did he learn so much scripture in Nazareth? It is just a small town with few who know how to read or write. I even understand that the people there didn't accept him very well. Did you hear that too?"

"Yes, but prophets are not well accepted in their hometowns. History shows it. To grow up somewhere and then announce that God sends you is tough for the hometown boys to believe. If you told me you were a prophet, I would certainly balk!" Enoch chuckled.

"Hum, I guess you would."

"I did a lot of studying in Alexandria, Cleopas. Scripture is mysterious sometimes, and prophecy fulfilled over very long periods. Remember how long it took God to fulfill his promise to Abraham? He almost lost Isaac in the process! It is not clear to me either, what promise lies in these events, but surely the world is changed. You heard the gentile, Justin, call Simeon 'Brother' didn't you?"

"Yes, it is an expression often used by Jesus when he spoke of his followers. Possibly that is where Justin got the idea. It sure seems strange to me," replied Cleopas.

"Jesus called God 'Father' too. Did you ever hear him say that?"

"No, I didn't hear that. Did he really?"

"Yep."

They walked in silence for a long while. Both contemplated the idea of Jesus calling God, Father. Neither would do such a thing! Yet, Jesus spoke with such authority and honesty that perhaps there was more to it than just a phrase. Abraham was the Father of the Jews. Perhaps he was speaking to Abraham and not God. They could not quite remember. It saddened them that already they were not remembering *exactly* what he said.

They passed other slower travelers along the path until they caught up with a man about their age who matched their pace and tagged along as they discussed their theories. Neither noticed him much but didn't mind the stranger joining them.

"How will we ever know what it means?" commented Enoch. "He came and taught us so well, and yet he disappeared nearly as quickly as he came."

"His death was certainly based on a trumped-up charge and a mock trial. I think of Nadab sometimes, and I boil inside. That ambitious liar! He was a part of it and did nothing to stop it even after knowing what Jesus did for my brother! How could he do such a thing?" Enoch spit on the ground.

Cleopas said, "Nadab was probably duped."

"I don't know, Cleopas. He wanted so much to be an important part of the temple politics that it was inevitable he would do something stupid," Enoch chided.

"Well, if he was part of a conspiracy to kill the Messiah, he is *doomed*," offered Cleopas.

"I guess," said Enoch with finality, spitting again.

All this time the stranger said nothing. Enoch and Cleopas looked over at him, but his eyes remained straight ahead, and he did not notice the stare. He kept an even pace and walked without tiring. Not to be outdone, Enoch and Cleopas pressed on.

Cleopas spoke next. "Where were we? He was born in the right place. That is not much to go on. We need to do better than that!"

"You are right. All that study in Alexandria, and all I can think of is that he was to be a savior and was born in the right town. I know he cured my brother, that's for sure. No one could have done that but a prophet or the Messiah. So at least he is a prophet. Yet, no prophet rose from the dead, did he? If this is true, I can believe," responded Enoch. Exhausted, they stopped for a while and stood still. The stranger stopped also.

Finally, the stranger turned to the two and asked, "What are you discussing together as you walk along?"[21]

Cleopas and Enoch stood there with their faces downcast and without looking up, Cleopas replied, "Are you only a visitor to Jerusalem and don't know the things that have happened there in these days?"

"What things?" he asked.

"About Jesus of Nazareth," Cleopas replied. "He was a prophet, powerful in word and deed before God and all the people. The chief priests and our rulers handed him over to be sentenced to death, and they crucified him; but we had hoped that he was the one who was going to redeem Israel. And what is more, it is the third day since all this took place. In addition, some of our women amazed us. They went to the tomb early this morning but didn't find his body. They came and told us that they had seen a vision of angels, who said he was alive. Then some of our companions went to the tomb and found it just as the women had said, but him they did not see."[22]

"He said he could raise the temple in three days. Well he did it, but they thought he was talking about the

[21] Luke 24:17, NIV
[22] Luke 24:18-24, NIV

temple in the city. That would have certainly been much easier," chimed in Enoch.

Then the stranger said to them, "How foolish you are, and how slow of heart to believe all that the prophets have spoken! Did not the Christ have to suffer these things and then enter his glory?"[23] He had turned to them and there before them was Jesus himself, but still they didn't recognize him!

Then Jesus began to walk, and they walked along, one on each side, gazing intently and listening to every word he spoke. Then Jesus began explaining to them what was said in all the scripture concerning the Messiah, beginning with Moses and all the prophets.

As they approached the village to which they were going, Jesus acted as if he were going farther. But they urged him strongly, "Stay with us, for it is nearly evening; the day is almost over." So, he went in to stay with them.[24]

Cleopas handed over the satchel to the courier at the inn, and his work was complete. Wanting to hear more, they invited the stranger to supper with them. They bought some bread, wine and cheese from the innkeeper and sat at an empty table outside under an olive tree for supper. Then, Jesus stood, and took the bread, gave thanks, broke it and reached across the table to give it to them. As Jesus handed

---

[23] Luke 24:24-26, NIV
[24] Luke 24:28-29, NIV

them the broken pieces of bread, Enoch and Cleopas saw his hands for the first time. As they took the bread from his hands, they saw the punctures. They could hardly believe their eyes and wanted to grab his hands but were afraid. Their eyes slowly shifted to Jesus' eyes as he drew back across the table and stood erect again. Then their own eyes were opened, and they recognized him! Their eyes were wide with amazement as they reclined there at the table.

They didn't know whether to rise to their feet or fall on their faces. Then, in a flash of light, he disappeared from their sight! They turned to each other and Enoch asked, "Were not our hearts burning within us while he talked with us on the road and opened the Scriptures to us?"[25] Cleopas could not speak. He was too awe struck.

They rose from the table, thanked the innkeeper and headed back to Jerusalem almost giddy with excitement as Enoch chattered all the way. Enoch and Cleopas no longer doubted the empty tomb or that Jesus was, indeed, the Messiah. "Simeon will be so happy to hear our news!" exclaimed Enoch.

Cleopas finally regained enough composure to speak. "They will all cheer. This is enormous, Enoch. I believed he was a prophet, but he is truly the Messiah. There is no doubting it now. The resurrection of the Messiah surpasses the feasts and festivals. I just don't know what it means to us Jews, much less gentiles like Justin."

---

[25] Luke 24:32, NIV

Enoch and Cleopas went directly to the shop but withheld the good news. Simeon knew they were excited and obviously home much earlier than they had predicted. All they wanted to know was how to get to Jesus' followers. Simeon told them the whereabouts of the eleven close followers of Jesus and, knowing the way, Simeon joined them. Little Jacob followed as they rushed to the small upper room while trying to pace themselves to avoid suspicion.

When they arrived, they found James and John with their mother and Simon, called Peter, the rest of the eleven and about ten other followers. The room was quite full. Peter explained that it was true, that Jesus had risen and appeared to him. Then Cleopas and Enoch explained what had happened on the road to Emmaus, and how they recognized Jesus when he broke the bread.

Everyone was ecstatic! The defeat had turned to victory for the believers. Never in history had such a thing happened. Jesus had shown the way!

As the crowd settled down, Peter came over to Enoch, Simeon and Little Jacob. "You know that Jesus came to reconcile us with God and with each other don't you?"

"Yes, we see that *now*," replied Simeon.

Peter continued, "We will be staying here in Jerusalem for a while. Jesus wanted us to stay here, so we will do as he says. Pray for us. We need encouragement and friends like you. I know of you, Simeon, because I remember the day you were healed. What a wonderful experience for all of us! It is good to see you again. And this is your brother?"

"Yes, this is Enoch of Bethlehem, my brother."

"Thank you for explaining what you saw on the road to Emmaus. It reinforces what we now know."

"I am humbled to meet you, Simon...uh... Peter," Enoch stumbled.

"And who is this young one?" asked Peter as he looked down at Little Jacob.

"This is Jacob of Jerusalem, my adopted son," replied Simeon.

Little Jacob looked up at Peter and nodded. Then he looked at Simeon, and held his arms out. Simeon gave Little Jacob the hug of a lifetime, while both felt a little dampness come to their eyes.

Cleopas and Enoch stayed behind a little longer, as Simeon and Little Jacob bid Peter and the others farewell and headed back to the pottery shop.

Simeon looked down at Little Jacob, "Come, Jacob, the world awaits us!"

Continue

THE BROTHERS SERIES
with these books!

JERUSALEM'S BROTHERS
&
BROTHERS FOREVER

Available at:
Your local bookstore
Amazon.com
Or
PageTurner.us
Visit my website: RonaldHera.com

Printed in the USA
CPSIA information can be obtained
at www.ICGtesting.com
LVHW052055290823
756437LV00001BB/125